Fat Girl Slim

Marina Johnson

DEDICATION

For PG and CJ, who again made it possible.

Also by Marina Johnson

A Confusion of Murders

Chapter 1

The first time I saw Bella she was frowning and she looked to be in an almighty hurry. She was marching with rapid, clip-cloppity steps that echoed importantly on the supermarket floor. She had her head down, deep in thought so she didn't notice me studying her, but no one ever notices me. At least, not in a good way.

It was four o'clock on a murky January afternoon and I was on my usual circuit of the Foodco aisles thinking about the miserable Christmas Mother and I had just had. Bella was tugging along one of those new hand baskets on wheels, very chic looking but not nearly big enough for everything I wanted to buy, and I just happened to look up and there she was. I guessed she'd just finished work because she was wearing one of those lanyards with a security pass swinging from it, somehow managing to make even that look glamorous, all swingy and important. That's how I knew her name, Bella Somerton, isn't that a beautiful name? If she wanted to be an actress she wouldn't even need to change her name, it's just perfect as it is. Sales manager, Brotherton Estate Agents, it stated on the lanyard. I don't think she noticed me staring at her and reading it. My body might be slow and cumbersome but I can read very quickly.

I wish I had a lanyard but I'd need to get a job first, although on second thoughts perhaps not; no chance of a lanyard swinging anywhere on me, it'd be lost in the rolls of fat. And my name wouldn't look half as good as hers; Alison Travis, it would say, *unimportant fat person and dogsbody.*

Destiny, that's what it was, although I didn't realise that at the time. I'd seen a black cat that morning and I waited and waited to make sure it crossed my path so I knew it was going to be a lucky day. I just looked at her and *wished* that I could be like her and have a life like hers. Although I didn't even know anything about her life then but I knew it would be far, far better than mine. And it was fate, or serendipity or whatever you want to call it because we did meet months later, so that just shows it was meant to be.

But still, I'll never forget seeing her that first time. Her long hair was billowing behind her in a lovely white blonde cloud and even though she was frowning she still looked flawless. Two faint horizontal lines of concentration between her eyes only served to make her seem thoughtful and more interesting. No, nothing could spoil that perfect face and figure.

Seems strange to remember something like that, doesn't it? There are lots of pretty girls around if you care to look, oodles of girls who've hit every pretty branch on their way down to earth. But looking back it was a sign, an omen, because we did meet properly eventually, even though, obviously, she didn't remember me. I like to think of that moment when I first saw her as my rebirth, the start of the new me, my new life. Although I had no intention of making the changes immediately as I'd just bought myself a nice big packet of milk chocolate digestives and a six pack of cheese and onion crisps and there was no way I was going to waste them. Or so I thought at the time.

So, I sort of followed her. Okay, I *did* follow her and I admired her from afar (the health food aisle actually, not that *I* was going to buy anything from it) and I had to speed up to keep pace with her as she walks very quickly. I was a bit out of breath to be honest; then I queued up and collected Mother's weekly prescription from the chemist counter and then went to the checkout to pay for my shopping. The checkout was near to the self-scan checkouts and as I was waiting I could see Bella putting her shopping through the till and she even did that very prettily. Once I'd paid I bagged all of my shopping up and lumbered out to the car park. The cashier watched me stuff everything into bags and made no offer of help at all. I had a feeling the sheer size of me annoyed her and it might have been my imagination but every time she scanned something fattening she sniffed.

When I got outside I looked for Bella in the car park but she must have gone and I remember I was disappointed; I wanted to know what kind of car she drove. If that cashier had helped me I might have got out there in time. And then I got in my car and went home to cook dinner just like any other day. Pork chops and mashed potatoes.

Except.

Something clicked in my brain that day and I made up my mind there and then; no more time wasting, no more being pathetic, *I* was going to become just like Bella. I'd made promises like that to myself so many times but this time I meant it. I was going to have a life before I was too old to enjoy it. Before it was too late.

I wasn't going to tell mother though because she'd only say I was being silly and to be satisfied with what I'd got. Be grateful for all of the sacrifices she'd made for me.

No. It was going to be my little secret. It'd take a while before I could put my plan into action – I had to work on Mother for one thing. And my plan was a bit vague to be honest. I knew it would have to involve getting a job of some sort but I just had this feeling that things would work out, somehow. And I needed to let Mother think that everything was her idea otherwise I'd have no chance of it working. I've made that mistake too many times; got all excited about something that I wanted to do and Mother's seemingly gone along with it, and then, bang, right at the last minute she'd change her mind and I'd be left devastated. It's for my own good, Mother would say, it's all very well having these silly ideas about jobs and things but who's left to pick up the pieces when it all goes wrong? Well, Mother, of course.

And anyway, she'd say, why do you want to get a job or to meet new people when everything you need is right here in this house, don't you have everything a person could possibly want?

No. This time I'm going to be a bit clever and let Mother think it was her idea, and then *maybe* it'll work.

'You've put too much salt in these potatoes. And the chops are overcooked.' Mother's thin lips turn down at the corners and she frowns. Her tightly permed curls move slightly with the effect; she wouldn't do that if she knew how unflattering it looks. Sort of like a grey woolly hat being tightened. I think I might have to use bigger rollers next time I perm it.

'Sorry.'

Mother puts her knife and fork down and pushes the tray away with a slight sneer of disgust.

'I'll just have some pudding.'

This isn't a good sign. Maybe I wasn't concentrating when I was cooking because I was too busy thinking about how I'm going to change my life. Or she could just be looking for an excuse. I have to tread carefully otherwise the overcooked chops could blow up into a huge row which lasts the whole night. Which means I'll miss my programmes.

'I can make you something else, Mother.' I pick the tray up from the bed.

'No. I'll just have pudding.'

'Okay.' I turn to come out of her room and down the stairs.

'Can't wait to get away, can you?'

And that's when I know that it's pointless, she's going to *start* and there's no stopping it.

'I'm not made of money you know,' she says,' I can't afford for you to be wasting food like that.'

I stop and turn around but I know it's too late. I know now that there'll be no programmes for me tonight, she's going to have one of her *episodes*. That black cat wasn't so lucky after all.

'I'm really sorry Mother.'

'Hmm.' Mother pulls the quilt tighter around her. 'It's okay for you, living here for nothing, everything provided for you. You don't even have to work. I worked for years, you'd don't know how lucky you are. I don't think you appreciate everything I do for you.' Her voice is increasing in volume and I'm grateful that we have no neighbours to hear.

When she's like this it makes no difference what I say, she won't be placated however hard I try. I did make the mistake once of thinking I might as well vent how *I* feel if she's just to going to carry on anyway. Big, big mistake, it was months before she forgave me, months of nit-picking and checking every penny that I spent, every minute I was out of the house. It was absolutely unbearable and I learned from that mistake and never did it again.

'Most people your age would be out earning a living.' She almost shouts at me. It's true, but I'm not most people, am I? I've never even had a job. After my A levels I intended to go to university to study English; I'd applied and been offered a place but then Mother had her stroke so I had to put it off. I was so disappointed. Especially when I saw all of my old school friends leaving for their new lives. The university let me defer it to the following year but Mother was still too ill for me to go and eventually I gave up the place and that was that. I've looked after her ever since. Ten years.

'Selfish, like your father. He didn't care either.'

'Of course I care, Mother, you know I do.'

'He left me. I expect you want to leave too, don't you? Well, go on, I'm not stopping you. I can pay someone to look after me, probably cost less than keeping *you*.'

She can't help it, that's what I tell myself. Most of

6

the time she's alright. Okay, she's not alright she's just about bearable. But every few weeks we have a blow up like this. Tonight, it was the potatoes and the chops but it could be anything. Last time I didn't iron her nightie properly. It's just an excuse; a reason to explode at me. In my kinder moments I excuse her behaviour by reasoning that it's frustration. But in my unkind moments I think she does it because she enjoys it.

I stand mutely in the doorway, it's completely pointless to try and argue with her. It just has to run its course; first we'll have the insults, the shouting, then I'll have to apologise, then the tears.

'You can leave anytime you like, I'm not stopping you – you go right ahead, see if you can find someone else to give you a home.'

I'm used to it now and her words have no power to hurt me. She knows that I've nowhere else to go, no friends that I could stay with.

'You,' she points her finger at me, 'are a fat lump and you need to do something about your eating because it's not healthy, the amount you eat.'

I am a fat lump and she doesn't even know the half of what I eat. On a normal evening I'll go downstairs after I've seen to Mother and watch my soaps and quiz programmes and I can eat and eat as much as I like without her knowing. Comfort eating, it's called, although I don't know why it's called that because I get no comfort from it at all. It's more of a compulsion. Something that I *have* to do.

And because Mother can't get down the stairs I know that I'm safe. I take her cocoa and her biscuits up to her at nine thirty and then I have peace until seven o'clock the next morning. She usually falls asleep around ten and very rarely bothers me. Occasionally I'll be summoned to help her to the toilet but usually she'll go to sleep. She can just about get to her en-suite on her own using her walking frame but she insists I help her. She calls me upstairs and I have to wait outside the door like a servant until she's finished. I'm sure she does it because she knows I hate it

'And I'm only saying that for your own good, because I care about you.' She's still going on. I don't reply; I have an expression that I fix on my face which I hope conveys that I'm listening and she's right. I don't need to listen to what she's saying because it's always the same. I'll wait for her to wear herself out and then I'll make my escape downstairs.

'It's not healthy being that size, maybe you should go back to the doctor to give you a diet sheet.'

I nod. That's what I do, I agree with everything she says. Last year she went on about my weight so much I made an appointment to see the doctor and he encouraged me to join a slimming club. He also said he thought I was depressed although I didn't tell Mother that because I'd never hear the end of it. It was strange, when I made the appointment I felt sure I'd be made to feel like a fat, lazy pig by the doctor but it wasn't like that at all; quite the opposite in fact which is why I started crying and he thought I was depressed. It was the unexpected kindness you see, I'm not used to it.

Anyway, I came home and told Mother about the slimming club and she could see straight away that I didn't want to do it so of course she absolutely insisted that I went to the meeting at the community centre. I didn't want to go and I couldn't even lie and pretend I'd been because I knew she'd want to see the pamphlets and diet plan the minute I got home. I was so nervous that I couldn't eat my tea before I went; the food just wouldn't go down which is unheard of for me.

I remember walking into the hall and being shocked at the amount of people in there, people as fat, and fatter, than me. For once I didn't feel out of place and embarrassed about my size. A bubbly dark-haired lady saw me standing by the door and came over and introduced herself as Fiona, the group leader. She took my hand and led me over to the table at the front. I had a moment of panic then, I thought maybe I'd have to be weighed in front of everyone, but no, it was all very discreet, no one ever knows what you weigh, and she even asked me how much weight I wanted to lose! No lectures, no telling me what to do, Fiona said it didn't work like that, that's not what they're there for.

No one sniggered as I followed Fiona to the front, no wide-eyed looks like I get from people as I waddle into Foodco with my trolley, no pursed lips like I get when I put my chocolate and crisps through the check-out (I use the self-service when possible now, much better).

No, my fellow weight watchers smiled and said *hello,* they welcomed me.

The hour and a half just flew by and I was sorry when the meeting finished; it was so nice to talk to other people without feeling judged. Actually, it was nice to talk to other people, full stop. Most days the only person I talk to is Mother or a shop assistant if they're not looking down their nose at me. People were even *laughing* about secret eating and binging on chocolate, instead of feeling guilty and disgusting for stuffing their faces. I even thought, maybe I can make some friends.

Of course when I came home I made the mistake of telling Mother all about it when I should have just kept my mouth shut. I should have known what would happen but I was so excited and pleased about the meeting that I couldn't help it. I was on a high and I forgot myself; I forgot to be careful. I was so looking forward to the next meeting, I couldn't wait for the week to go by and Mother never said anything and I thought, maybe, just maybe, I've got away with it.

So, I went to the next meeting and it was so lovely when I walked in and people remembered me and smiled and said hello. Miraculously, when I got onto the scales I'd actually lost five pounds. I was elated and I just couldn't wipe the smile off of my face. Anne, the lady sitting next to me said I should enjoy the feeling because that would keep me motivated to keep doing it. She'd lost three stone. Three stone! I started to think that maybe I could do it too. Anne said it was really important to stay for the 'fat talk' as she called it. Although a lot of people just came to get weighed, she said she always stayed. She promised to save me the seat next to her if I was going to stay every week, because she always sat in the front row. I felt a bit choked that someone would save a seat for me; not much to most people but it meant a lot to me.

But it didn't last. Fiona, the group leader, was just starting the fat talk when my phone started vibrating. It was Mother of course, ringing from the extension in her bedroom. I ignored it the first time but she rang again so I had to slip outside to take the call. I knew I couldn't ignore her again or it would result in one of her episodes. She sounded frail and pathetic and said she wasn't feeling very well at all so I had to go home immediately. I never even went back inside to say goodbye; I knew there was no point, I wouldn't be going there again.

Mother looked fine when I got home, quite recovered. I knew there was nothing wrong with her. Mother said perhaps it wasn't a good idea for me to go anymore as she didn't like being left on her own in the evenings; she felt vulnerable, was afraid she'd have a bad turn and I wouldn't get home in time. She said that since I had all the information I didn't need to go to the meetings to know how to do the diet. No point in wasting five pounds every week just to get weighed.

So, I had to agree with her, didn't I? I had no choice. And, of course, I put that five pounds back on by the next week and I've piled on even more since then.

So that was that. And I know Mother can't help it, but sometimes, you know, I think I'd like to kill her.

Chapter 2

Mother finally stopped her histrionics at nine o'clock and graciously allowed me to make her a cup of cocoa. I took it up to her with two rich tea biscuits and kissed her goodnight. We've agreed that I'll try harder to contain my nastiness and be more grateful for all that she does for me.

I come back downstairs and hover in the hallway until I'm sure she's asleep. It doesn't take long as she's worn herself out. I go into the lounge and close the curtains, shut the door quietly and turn the television on. I flop down onto the sofa with a big sigh of relief and flip through the menu until I find the recordings of Coronation Street. I turn the sound down low so it's a comforting background murmur. My mouth starts to water at the sight of the crisps and chocolate digestives which I've placed in readiness on the coffee table.

Secret eating, something Mother knows nothing about although she must know that I didn't get to be this size by eating the same as her. There are lots of things that Mother doesn't know about; I have a whole host of things that I keep from her.

I savour the anticipation of eating by delaying it a little longer and I pull my laptop onto my lap and turn it on. Mother doesn't know that I have a laptop, in fact she doesn't even know that we have broadband or wifi. The big, big plus about her not being able to get down the stairs is that she only knows what I want her to know.

For instance; she thinks that I'm totally dependent on her for money, that I have no income of my own at all.

Quite wrong.

I claim carers allowance for looking after her and she has no idea. If she did, she'd make me give it to her for rent as she never lets me forget that I live here for nothing. So I applied for it, got it and it goes straight into my own bank account which she also knows nothing about. It's enabled me to buy things for myself that I couldn't possibly have otherwise and has saved my sanity; it's a very limited secret life but without it I think I'd be dead.

Mother *does* give me twenty pounds a week pocket money to spend all on myself which she says is very generous as everything is provided so what could I possibly need money for? Twenty pounds barely covers my crisps, chocolate and the like. I can't buy my treats on the normal food bill because she would spot them instantly when she scrutinises the receipts. She also pays for a mobile phone for me, the most basic model available. It's for her benefit, the mobile phone, so she can call me if I'm not at home. The house phone is the only number in the contact list. Mother won't have a mobile phone, she says they warp the brain.

Mother receives a state pension and also a very good income from something called a *bond* although she has never admitted this to me, and she also gets benefits because of her condition, but every penny that I spend on shopping has to be accounted for. She scrutinises every receipt when I return and every bill that comes in. She gives me her debit card to pay for things but she won't allow me to be named on her account.

I only know about all of the money she has because of another little secret of mine; I have access to her accounts. I set it all up online and when the letter of confirmation arrived from the bank it never got to her because I opened it myself.

I open up the browser and log on to check her balance. She has over ten thousand pounds in her current account and that's without all of the savings accounts she has. Plus, she owns this house outright; inherited from my grandparents. It may be old fashioned and run down but it's in a semi-rural location and is detached with a huge garden, so is worth a tidy sum. I Googled similar houses and even allowing for the work that needs doing the amount it's worth made me gasp.

She always tells me she's poor but I'd guessed she was lying. Lying is her default; Mother basically lies about everything. Whenever her bank statement came she'd make sure to not let me see it so for a while I was stumped as to how I was going to find out. I couldn't even pretend it hadn't arrived because it always comes around the seventh of each month and if she didn't get it she'd ring the bank. In desperation I steamed a statement open but when I tried to reseal the envelope it was obvious it'd been opened. I contemplated throwing it away but then she'd have had to ring the bank for a copy. In the end I took it out in the garden, put it on the floor, put my foot on it and scuffed it around a bit. Then I gave it to her with the rest of the post which also got the scuffed around the garden treatment and I told her it came through the door like it. I *think* she believed me even though she looked at me in her usual suspicious way.

It was worth doing because before I put it back in the envelope I took a photograph of it on my phone which is how I applied for online banking. Much easier than trying to steam open envelopes.

I'm not making Mother sound very nice, am I? And I probably don't sound very nice either but that's because I've learned from the best. Mother.

Maybe I'm being a bit unfair about Mother because she's always looked after me, done her best for me in her own way. It's just that I feel so trapped. It's not her fault that she's ill. If I had a life of my own, some friends even, I wouldn't feel quite so resentful.

I wasn't always so fat and friendless, a bit chubby maybe, but I had friends at school, I had ambitions and I had a normalish life, although I was never allowed to bring friends home from school. Mother couldn't be doing with it, she said. The thing is, if you're never allowed to invite anyone round then people start to think you're a bit weird and stop inviting you. So it makes it awkward to have friends, but I did have some. For a while.

I know this sounds completely stupid and impossible but sometimes I think how convenient it was that Mother had her stroke just when I was about to leave home and go to university. And that's ridiculous, isn't it? It's not as if she could make herself have a stroke is it? Although she was only sixty-three, which is very young for a stroke. And she didn't smoke, or drink and she wasn't overweight so she was just very unlucky and by association so was I. She's only seventy-three now, so she could easily live another twenty years or more.

I never knew my father as he'd gone before I was even born. Mother doesn't talk about him very much, usually just to say how selfish and gutless he was, leaving her in the lurch. And that I'm just like him and got all of his bad personality traits and none of her good ones. I must have been an accident, a mistake, no one in their right mind would get pregnant at forty-five, would they? I'm pretty sure that she couldn't have realised she was pregnant until it was too late otherwise she'd have got rid of me. I can't imagine Mother having sex; I can't imagine any man wanting to have sex with Mother or even wanting to be around her to be honest.

I'm most likely biased; maybe she's nicer to other people than she is to me but I have no way of knowing as we never see anyone else, except for people who try to sell us stuff. She doesn't even see a doctor; her repeat prescriptions go straight to the pharmacy at Foodco. I think the last time Mother saw a doctor was three years ago when she had the flu, the doctor was in and out of the house in ten minutes and that included writing the prescription.

For most people getting pregnant at forty-five would be a disaster but luckily for Mother she has this house. We've lived here all of my life and most of hers. The grandparents must have left her quite a lot of money too because although she likes to say she's always worked, the truth is that she worked a couple of days a week at the library and there's no way that she could have lived on the wages from there.

I've never even seen a photograph of my father; mother says she doesn't have any so I have no idea what he looks like. I thought she might have been lying about not having a photograph but believe me I've searched this house from top to bottom and I can't find one. I think maybe I look like him because I look nothing like Mother. I've scoured the photograph album and I can't see that I look anything like my grandparents either. Tall, thin and miserable looking best describes my relatives, they definitely look like they eat to live and not live to eat. Mother even leaves food on her plate from the miniscule portions I serve her. I definitely don't take after her. I wonder if my father was fat?

I check Mother's current account and I'm not surprised to see that the balance has increased; we live so frugally that she's *saving* money. I log out and push the laptop off my lap and onto the sofa.

I feel unsettled; it's not the row with Mother, they don't even bother me now because it's always the same thing and I'm almost bored by the arguments.

I stare at the coffee table and the snacks waiting for me; I could watch my programmes now, they're all recorded and ready. Do the usual, settle on the sofa and binge watch and binge eat. I usually shovel it in and I can't settle until I've eaten every single thing. Then an overwhelming feeling of self-disgust will come over me and I'll vow that I'll never do it again. That feeling will last for about two hours and will gradually fade and if there's anything snack-like left in the house I'll then eat that. I've read loads about eating disorders and what I do is sort of like bulimia only I can't bear to be sick so maybe I'm just a fat, greedy pig. Eating your problems, I've read it's called. Maybe I should eat Mother.

No, I decide. I'm not going to stuff my face. I heave myself up from the sofa and snatch the crisps and biscuits from the table and march out to the kitchen, pausing briefly at the bottom of the stairs to listen for any movement from Mother's room. All quiet.

I continue to the kitchen but once I reach it I stand in the middle of the room, unsure what to do. The kitchen is unchanged from my childhood; orange laminated worktops and green painted cupboards. Seventies retro some would call it, to me it's hideous, depressing, dated and battered, the worktop has so many chips in it that it must be a health hazard. Mother could easily afford a new kitchen but she won't spend any money unless she absolutely has to.

I clutch the crisps and biscuits to my body and consider what to do. I want to stuff them into the bin in a grand gesture to show myself that I'm turning over a new leaf and I'm not going to eat them but I know from past experience that I'll probably be pulling them out again tomorrow.

Besides, I'd have to empty the overflowing bin first.

Another secret from Mother.

There isn't a spare inch of worktop space in the kitchen, dirty plates, cutlery and cups litter every available surface. I haven't washed up for three days and my normal routine is to only ever do so when I run out of crockery. Five days is my personal best but I cheated a bit as I gave Mother microwave meals for two of those days.

Another of my secrets.

Mother doesn't approve of microwaves, *wouldn't give one house room*. She certainly wouldn't eat such a thing as a microwave meal; not knowingly anyway. Fortunately, once I've dished it up on a plate and overcooked it a bit so it resembles my cooking, she has no idea she's eating one. I have to be a bit careful when I give her the shopping receipts though; I daren't buy them from Foodco as they give itemised receipts there which is a nightmare because Mother puts her reading glasses on and checks every single item. I can't get anything past her. The Indian mini-mart in the town centre is the place to go, they're not interested in giving itemised receipts so I get the microwave meals from there and pretend the receipts are for something else.

I have to make sure the kitchen door is shut when I cook them so there's no possibility of her hearing the ding of the microwave. She makes out she's deaf but you can never tell with Mother; I'm not sure how deaf she really is or if she's even deaf at all.

Oh yes, there's a lot Mother doesn't know and never will know as long as I can dissuade her from getting a stair lift. Every couple of months she says she's going to get one; the adverts are on TV the *whole* time. This usually results in a few anxious weeks for me while I persuade her not to get one, without her *knowing* I'm persuading her obviously; which means I have to encourage her and seem really keen for her to do something which has the opposite effect. It's exhausting.

Mother's extremely mean so the cost was enough to put her off last time; she kept on so much I rang up the company and they sent a salesman out to measure up and he then sent us a quote. He wanted Mother to sign up there and then but thankfully was really vague about the price which put Mother's back up. Mother had to be got out of bed and showered and dressed before he came, I even had to wash and set her hair. Then she insisted on being seated in her armchair in her room and I had to cover her bed with a big checked blanket to make it look less like a bed, apparently that's not decent, and all this had to be done before he arrived at ten o'clock.

All pretty pointless as the very fact we were considering a stair lift indicated that she was bed bound. But that's Mother for you.

When I was letting him out of the front door I let him know that Mother was loaded and would only want the very best so he'd be sure to quote for the deluxe model. Mother went into a rage when she finally saw the inflated quote and that salesman's name was mud, I can tell you. I could have bought a new car for the price of that stair lift. Although before she got the quote he was the best thing since sliced bread.

The salesman kept ringing up for weeks afterwards to try and get the sale and I was afraid to leave the house for a while in case he rang while I was out and Mother answered the extension in her bedroom. I couldn't have her knowing that he'd quoted for the most expensive stair lift they had. Every time the phone rang I'd jump and then race to the phone before Mother picked it up, it was awful. I had to be rude to him in the end to stop him ringing and he got a bit nasty, implied that we were time wasters. I told him if he rang again I'd report him to his boss and then I put the phone down on him. Served him right; he barely spoke to me while he fawned all over mother; made jokey comments about weight limits on stair lifts and would Mother be the only one using it, all the while giving me snide looks.

I just wish they'd stop advertising them on TV, because you never know with Mother, she might suddenly get it into her head that she wants to come downstairs, no matter what the cost and then where will we be? She'll be watching and inspecting everything I do and I'll have no peace at all.

So, to wash up or not to wash up? The kitchen looks pretty rank and to be honest I feel a bit disgusted with myself. Or shall I just go and sit down and eat those crisps and biscuits to cheer myself up?

I turn around to go and resume my place on the sofa when the image of Bella pops into my head and I stop in the doorway. Would she sit and stuff her face and generally behave like a slob? I can't imagine for a moment that she would, I'm certain that her house is just as perfect as she is. The thought of Bella lifts my spirits for some bizarre reason and a sprig of hope start to grow inside me and a little voice tells me that it's not too late.

Decision made I throw the crisps and biscuits onto the floor, stamping carefully on the crisps so that they don't explode and then I open the swing bin and pull out the overflowing liner. Once it's out of the bin I manage to stuff the crisps and biscuits inside and tie it in a double knot. I open the back door and drag it out to the dustbin and shove it inside. I close the lid and stand for a moment; it's freezing, the cold permeates the soles of my slippers and I shiver. Remember this moment, I tell myself, remember this moment because it's the first step in the making of the new me.

I go back into the kitchen, close and lock the door and survey the wreckage. Bella would never live like this and I decide that I will behave like her. I put another liner in the bin and scrape the leftovers off the plates and make a space so I can pile them up by the sink. An hour later and everything is washed and put away and the kitchen looks a lot tidier. But it looks dirty so I fill the sink up again, find a bottle of spray kitchen cleaner and start squirting and scrubbing the worktops and cupboards. By the time I've finished it's gone twelve o'clock and my eyes are drooping but I feel exhilarated; I've managed to not stuff my face all evening and I've cleaned the kitchen so that it sparkles and I actually feel quite proud of myself. I'm just about to reward myself with something nice to eat when I remember that I don't do that anymore.

No. I will not give in.

I heave myself up the stairs, pausing at the door to Mother's room to listen. I gently push her door open to the muted sound of her TV and snoring. I step across the room and turn it off then remove her glasses from her face before she crushes them in her sleep and place them carefully in their case on her bedside table.

I come out and pull the door nearly closed and pad

along the landing to the bathroom. As I brush my teeth over the salmon pink sink I appraise the bathroom; decidedly grubby. The acrylic bath has a nasty black ring around it and the toilet could definitely do with a scrub.

Tomorrow, I decide.

Tomorrow I will give the bathroom a spring clean; time to stop living like a slob.

Time to be more like Bella.

Chapter 3

When Mother's Daily Mail was shoved through the letterbox this morning by the spotty, sullen teenager from the newsagents, inside was a bunch of leaflets and flyers, the usual two for one on pizzas, a handyman for everything and other assorted junk mail. I usually throw it all straight into the bin, and that's exactly where it was going until a sheet of paper fell onto the floor as I was chucking them away and when I picked it up, the words jumped out at me.

Cleaners wanted! No experience necessary – hours to suit

Is this fate? Could this be another sign that there's going to be a new me. Could I actually get a job? I think it definitely is a sign because I dreamed I was on a rollercoaster last night and I checked my dream dictionary and it means I'm embarking on an exciting journey. Perhaps a cleaning job is the first step. I'm overqualified for cleaning even though I've never had a job. Even so, it's a start; it'll get me away from Mother and I can earn some money.

I put the rest of the pamphlets in the bin and place the flyer carefully back inside the newspaper while I get Mother's breakfast ready. I arrange her cornflakes and jug of milk carefully on the tray along with a cup of tea, tuck the newspaper underneath my arm and carry it up the stairs. Once she's eaten that I'll have to take her toast up to her; she doesn't like cold toast.

I place the tray and newspaper on her bedside table while I hook my arms under Mother's armpits and help her to sit up, plumping the pillows behind her.

'Ouch!' she glares at me as I pull her up, 'You're pinching me, you great lump.'

Her mood hasn't improved much since last night and I'm going to have to suffer several days of her nastiness.

Well, more nasty than normal.

'Sleep well, Mother?' I know better than to argue and give the pillow a final, satisfying pummel.

'No,' she snaps and lets out a deep sigh, 'never slept a wink, dreadful night.'

'Oh, dear, that's a shame.' I say sympathetically. She was snoring the whole night; I could hear her from my bedroom. I pull out the legs from underneath the tray and place it carefully over her lap.

'Tea's a bit weak.' She takes a miniscule sip from the cup and pulls a displeased face as she puts the cup back down.

'Sorry, I'll make the next one a bit stronger.'

Mother purses her lips and sniffs. I put the paper on the bed next to her so that the flyer slips out onto the quilt. I hurriedly pick it up and whisk it away and turn to go back downstairs.

'What's that you're hiding?' she says suspiciously, I stop with my back to her.

'Nothing. Just rubbish.' I allow myself a small smile.

'I'll be the judge of that, give it to me.'

I turn around with what I hope is a *caught me* expression and carry it back over and give it to her.

25

She takes the flyer from me and frowns as she reads it then looks up at me with an appraising look. She's trying to read my mind, find out why I was trying to hide it from her.

'Says no experience necessary,' she says.

'Oh, they always say that, Mother, and then when you ring them they always want loads.' I put my hand out to take it from her.

'Might be worth a phone call, you could fit a few hours in between looking after me.' She tightens her grip on the flyer.

'I expect the jobs are already gone.' My hand hovers in mid-air.

Mother puts her hands on her lap, keeping a firm hold of the flyer.

'We could do with the extra money. The way things are going up we're going to have to tighten our belts and cut down anyway.'

Liar.

I keep my face impassive; no need to overdo it.

'Ring them,' she commands, holding the flyer back out to me. I hesitate and she snatches it back. 'Or I can, if you're too frightened to speak to them.' She says nastily.

I reach across the bed and take the flyer from her fingers.

'No, I'll ring them Mother,' I say with what I hope is a worried expression, 'I'll let you know what they say.'

'And don't take all day about it either.' She picks the newspaper up, gives it a shake and starts to read. 'And I don't want to hear any of your excuses.'

She doesn't see the smile on my face as I come

down the stairs. Mission accomplished.

I put Mother's toast in the toaster and wait. I look around the kitchen with a feeling of pride, pleased with last night's work. I got up earlier than usual this morning and did some exercises.

Yes, really, I *exercised*.

I can't go to a gym for obvious reasons, I'm too fat and Mother wouldn't allow it so I thought: I'll jog. Not in public, at least not to start with because I probably won't even make it to the end of the lane. I shut the door of the lounge and started jogging on the spot, it sounded like an elephant was jumping up and down on the floor so I had to stop otherwise Mother would have been asking what was going on. I took my slippers off and tried again and it was much better; hardly any noise at all. Well, jogging on the spot might be easy to someone of normal size and normal fitness but after five minutes I was sweating, out of breath, my face was burgundy and I thought I was going to die. My legs were burning with the effort and I had to go and put some talcum powder on the tops of my legs afterwards because they'd chafed where they're rubbed together. But that'll pass, when they get thinner they won't rub together, will they?

I will persevere, I'll gradually increase it and it'll get easier. Afterwards, once I'd had a lie down on the sofa, I soon recovered. I did a few stretches and bends and if I do it whenever I can it's got to make a difference, hasn't it?

After that I cleaned the bathroom and when I'd finished I treated myself to a bubble bath and had a lovely long soak. Can't remember the last time I did that. I usually avoid long soaks in the bath because I

27

like to get showered and dressed as quickly as possible so I don't have to look at myself. But it's different now; I made myself have a good long look in the mirror because this is the old me, this is the fattest I'll ever be because I'm going to be slim. Like Bella. It wasn't pleasant looking at myself and I won't be taking any *before* selfies either. Just looking was bad enough.

Breakfast was a bit different, too. Usually I have a big bowl of muesli followed by three slices of toast topped with butter and peanut butter. This lasts me until around ten o'clock when I have a snack; a couple of packets of crisps and some chocolate digestives and maybe a slice of cake. Today my breakfast was forty grams of cornflakes with skimmed milk and a cup of coffee. I won't say it was easy; I felt as if I'd eaten two mouthfuls and it was gone. I know I'll have hunger pangs in about an hour but I'm going to use the pangs. Every time I get one I'll think: this means I'm losing weight. I'm not going to eat anything else until tonight when I have dinner. Whenever I'm tempted I'll think of Bella, and how much I want to be like her.

I suppose you could say she's my role model.

The toast pops and I put it on a plate and scrape a miniscule amount of butter over it, my mouth waters but I ignore it and take the plate upstairs to Mother.

'Rung them yet?' she barks at me as I put the toast on her tray.

It's definitely working; she won't let it drop now.

'Not yet, Mother, they're probably not open yet.' I pick up her cereal bowl.

'Of course they will be,' she snorts, 'it's quarter

past nine. You need to ring them *now*, get in early before all the jobs are gone.'

'Okay,' I say meekly, 'I'll ring them as soon as I get downstairs.'

Once I get downstairs, I go into the lounge and pick the phone up and dial the number on the leaflet.

'Good morning, Moppers Homeclean, how may I help?' The voice on the other end sounds disgustingly cheerful and upbeat.

'Hello,' I say in my best imitation of her jolly tone. 'I've seen your advertisement for cleaners and would like to apply.' I cross my fingers and hope that there are still vacancies.

'Wonderful,' she gushes, 'we do indeed have vacancies with hours to suit, as many or as few as you wish. Are you able to come into the office for an interview?'

'Yes, of course, when would you like me to come in?'

'Today? We need people to start as soon as possible. Are you employed at the moment?'

'Er, no, not at the moment.'

'Wonderful! Then you'll be able to start straight away, yes?"

'Immediately.' Could this get any better?

'Super. Can I take your name?'

'Alison Travis.'

'Okay Alison, shall we say two o'clock? Our office is just off the precinct.'

'Yes, two o'clock will be fine.' She's put the phone down before I've finished speaking but it doesn't dampen my mood; I have an interview!

My first thought is that I need to find something

29

suitable to wear and do something with my hair. I go back upstairs and into my bedroom and pull open the wardrobe doors. I have nothing decent to wear, I know that everyone says that but in my case it's true. My normal daily attire consists of long baggy tops to hide my enormous stomach and black leggings to squeeze my elephantine legs into. I pull out a long black blouse and black leggings. A new pair of unworn black velvet effect ballet pumps stare up at me from the bottom of the wardrobe. I bought them ages ago but have never worn them. My feet are too fat for them and they're agonising to wear but in desperation I try them on anyway. I cram my toes into the end and force my heel in. My foot feels as if it's in a vice and the middle of my foot bulges from the shoe in a big shiny mound. I walk across the room and it's agonising but I have nothing else to wear so I'll have to suffer. I can wear my old, shabby shoes to drive there and change them before I go in. If I park in the precinct it won't be too far to walk.

My hair. Shoulder length, good old British mouse is the best way to describe it. Flyaway and dead straight, I've never been able to do much with it and usually have it scraped back in a ponytail. I washed it this morning and it's nearly dry and I contemplate curling it but dismiss that idea instantly; the curl will drop the minute I step out of the house and it'll be a mass of frizz by the time I get to Moppers. No, it'll have to be a business-like ponytail; it's only a cleaning job after all. I peer into the mirror and scrutinise my face; hmm, not too bad.

Decent skin, small turned up nose which looks slightly piggish because I'm so fat but when I'm normal size it will look quite cute. Large eyes, green flecked with amber, and, though I say it myself, very long eyelashes. Definitely my best feature.

I rummage around in the top drawer of my chest of drawers which serves as a make-up box and pull out a dried up mascara. I throw that in the waste bin and rummage again and pull out a broken pallet of eye shadows. I yank the entire drawer out and swirl my hand around; a collection of dried up foundation, mushed lipsticks and oddments of eye shadow. I upend the drawer and tip it all into the bin. It's all at least ten years old and I don't know why I've even kept it as I never wear make-up.

I never go anywhere.

When I've lost weight, I'll buy new make-up to go with the new me.

I'll just have to go with the natural look for today; it's a cleaning job so they won't be expecting me to be dolled up.

'ALISON!' Mother shouts from her room, she must have heard me come upstairs.

'ALISON!'

'Coming Mother,' I shout back.

I go into her room and pick the tray up from the bed.

'Have you rung them? She demands.

'Who?' I pretend to not know who she means.

'The cleaning people, about the job. Have you rung them?'

'They were engaged,' I lie. 'I'll have to try later.'

Mother harrumphs loudly, 'Well mind you do or else I will.'

'Doing it now, Mother,' I call over my shoulder as

I walk down the stairs. 'Doing it now.'

I walk past Moppers Homeclean the first time and am at the end of the street when I realise I must have missed it. I retrace my steps slowly, and painfully, because the shoes are killing me. I wish I'd kept my shabby shoes on. I scrutinise the door numbers and stop in front of a huge shop window blanked out with grubby, dirty white vertical blinds. The copper coloured metal door next to it has a torn piece of cardboard with *Moppers Homeclean* written on it in thick black pen. The sign is taped to the inside of the glass on the door which is also smeared and misty.

I push the door open and enter a small office, grubby, grey carpet tiles cover the floor and there's a faint smell of cabbage. Not a good advertisement for a cleaning company. A huge battered desk is positioned more or less in front of the door and a woman is seated at it knitting what looks like a very complicated, multi coloured jumper which she hurriedly hides when she sees me.

'Can I help?' She looks at me with annoyance.

'Hi, I'm Alison Travis. I have an interview at two o'clock.' I paste a bright smile on my face.

'Take a seat.' She waves a hand at a threadbare chair to the right of the desk while looking longingly at her knitting which is peeking out from the bag she's stuffed it in. 'Veronica will be with you shortly.'

'Thanks.' I sit down gingerly on the rickety chair, unsure if it will hold my weight. I sit very still, hold my breath and hope for the best. The receptionist ignores me and shuffles some papers so I have a look around the office; directly behind her is a door marked *Manager* which I'm guessing is where Veronica is. I mentally measure the width between the desk and my chair and hope that I can squeeze through it to get to my interview.

The *Manager* door is suddenly flung open and a mini-skirted, spiky-haired, peroxide blonde comes out. Fake tanned and wearing shiny black plastic over the knee boots, she looks to be about my age. She stops at the desk and hands a piece of paper to the receptionist.

'My P45 from my last job, innit.'

The receptionist takes it from her and looks at me, 'You can go in now.' She nods in the direction of the *Manager* door.

I won't fit through the gap now the blonde is in the way; I know that without even trying. I'm wondering what to do when the receptionist looks at me again.

'You can go in,' she says a bit louder.

The blonde looks at me and I see her eyes drop down my body and take in the size of me and the realisation dawning on her that I won't fit through and the usual feeling of shame swamps me. Her eyes return to my face and I see a spark of sympathy in her eyes. My estimation of her goes up as she moves quietly out of the way so I can get through.

I murmur a *thanks* and she gives me a surprisingly sweet smile.

I step through into the manager's office which is even smaller than the outer office. Veronica is seated behind a slightly newer looking desk and has her head down as she fills in a weekly planner with a pen.

'Sit yourself down,' she says without looking up. 'I

won't be a moment.'

I squash myself into the chair and wait.

'Okay,' she says with a smile, 'you must be Alison.' The smile fades as she looks up from the desk at me.

I give her a minute to get over the shock of the immenseness of me.

'Hello,' I say, reaching across the desk to shake her hand. 'Nice to meet you, Veronica.'

She stares at my hand as if it were a snake about to sink its fangs into her and then recovers and reluctantly puts her hand out to shake mine. Perhaps she's afraid I'm going to crush it. 'You're interested in the cleaning job, is that right?'

'Yes I am. Very interested.'

'Okay,' she purses her lips. 'We do need people with experience, do you have any?'

'Oh yes, lots,' I lie.

'Who have you worked for?'

'Um. Well, not paid for work. But I clean my own house and my mother's. I'm her carer you see.'

'Hmm. I'm afraid that doesn't really count as experience.'

I can see where this is going and I don't like it, not one bit.

'But,' I say, trying to sound calm. 'Your advertisement said no experience required.'

She looks caught out; she wasn't expecting me to challenge her.

'Did it?' she thinks for a moment. 'Okay, what I'll do is put you on the waiting list because the thing is, we've had a huge response and we don't really need any more cleaners at the moment. I'll put you on the list and let you know if any vacancies come up.'

'Oh.'

'Yes.' She dismisses me with a cold smile. 'If you give your details to Moira on reception she'll put you on file.

My plans for the new me slither to the floor and I feel utterly dejected; a vision of a huge bar of Dairy Milk pops into my head but I push it angrily away.

'I don't think so.' My voice sounds strong and determined, not like me at all.

'You've plenty of vacancies.' I go on. 'That planner you're filling in is at least half empty.' I tap the planner in front of her.

'I'm sorry.' She sits back and folds her arms. 'I'm afraid that you're not what we're looking for. I'm the one doing the interview and my decision is final. I don't have to justify myself to you or anyone else.'

We stare at each other across the desk but I win and she averts her gaze first.

'Okay.' I heave myself, with difficulty, out of the chair. 'It's your decision of course, just as it's my decision to ring up the Frogham Herald and tell them that a local cleaning company discriminates against fat people.'

Her mouth drops open and she stares at me.

'There's not much news in Frogham at the moment,' I say with a smile, 'I'm sure a bit of fat shaming in the community will go down a treat.'

Chapter 4

I pull up outside home, kill the engine and then rest my head on the steering wheel and take a deep breath.

I can't believe what I just did. What I just *said*.

I'm never that outspoken, that *brave*.

Or that rude.

But it had the desired effect; on Monday morning at nine o'clock sharp I'm to report to the Moppers office where I will be inducted and 'buddied' with another cleaner who will show me the ropes. Veronica made it very clear to me that I will be on probation, if I don't 'cut the mustard' as she put it, I'll be out on my ear.

I feel exhilarated; *daring*. And I don't even know where it came from, all that Frogham Herald nonsense; I just opened my mouth and out it came, as if I'd planned it all in advance.

I knew exactly what Veronica was thinking: I'm fat, lazy, and my enormous hips will knock things over and they'll be breakages and complaints and hiring me would just be a complete nightmare. I could see it in her eyes because I see it every day; in so many eyes.

It's true, your average person equates being fat with being lazy. And thick. Being as fat as me means that I must spend all day lying around eating from morning until night to get to this size and I'm obviously too stupid to go on a diet and lose some weight. And because I'm so fat and lazy I don't even have a job because, obviously, that would interfere with my constant eating and I'm too thick to hold down a job anyway. I do eat too much and that's a fact, but I'm not stuffing my face twenty-four-seven. I want to tell the people that look at me in disgust *be careful, this could be you if you don't watch yourself* but they wouldn't believe me, no one believes that you can get to this size without setting out with that very goal in mind.

I didn't balloon to this size overnight and I don't stuff my face every minute of every day. A few years of eating a bit too much every day and you're several stones overweight. Then the motivation to go on a diet disappears because it'll take *so long* and before you know it you've given up even thinking about dieting and that's it; you've turned into a whopper.

Yes, I could see it all and I thought; no, you're not going to spoil my dream, I can do a crappy cleaning job as well as the next person and actually, Veronica, I'm probably better educated than you.

I'm quite liking this new me, this daring new me. Perhaps this is the person I would have been if Mother hadn't taken ill. When I'm thin I'm going to have a new personality to go with my new body; no more *I'm so sorry I'm fat, I don't deserve anything Alison.*

The beep of a horn disturbs my thoughts; Dolph from number three is waving at me as he zooms past in his car. I smile and put a hand up and wave in response as he drives by. He cut my hair for me once, long ago, just after I'd finished my A levels and still had hopes of going to uni. I bump into him occasionally at Foodco with his partner, Brian, but I avoid him if I see him first. Not because I don't like him; I don't like me, I don't like people seeing me like this, I'm ashamed of how I am. He's offered several times to come and do Mother's hair for her, cheer her up. He'd do it for free, he says, trying to be kind. I told him that she's a bit nervous of people, doesn't like strangers in the house. Put him off.

She doesn't like strangers in the house, that's true, but she'd be more than happy to have a free hairdo and then slag him off afterwards; she's horrifically homophobic. I know what it would be like – she'd embarrass me in front of him by referring to my weight and lack of friends in her mock concerned way and I'd just want to shrivel up and die. And, I'm pretty sure Dolph would be sympathetic and not nasty because he seems like a nice guy but that would be even worse; pity. There's definitely no point in having my hair done, I'd just feel even more ridiculous with a nice new haircut over my blimp body.

So no. That won't be happening.

We live out of the way here. Semi-rural, I suppose you'd call it, right on the outskirts of Frogham. Away from the busy streets and we don't have very many neighbours either. We're at the end of a lane with open fields on one side and a double garage sized gap on the other side and then there's a short terrace of five cottages. We're number six Duck Pond Lane but there's not a duck pond, or duck, in sight. Maybe there was a long time ago.

Mother has never had much to do with the neighbours – she thinks she's better than them as our house is quite large and detached and the rest of the street is terraced so she thinks she's lord of the manor. We have an enormous garden which could easily accommodate two more houses. We can't possibly hope to maintain it and I've more or less given up with it and the grass is so long it's gone to seed. Mother's too tight to pay for a gardener and is under the illusion that I cut the grass and keep it tidy.

Another reason why she absolutely cannot have a stair lift put in; I feel quite anxious imagining what she would say if she saw the state of it. I push the thought firmly away; pointless to worry about things that will never happen.

I'm not exactly friends with any of the neighbours but I always wave and try to appear approachable when I see any of them, which isn't very often as if I see them first I make sure that they don't see me. For a big 'un I can move pretty quickly when it suits.

Number five are newish arrivals; a young couple who zoom off to work every morning, her in her Fiat 500 and him in his Audi. They're both slim and attractive, always bobbing about in trendy gym wear or helmeted up, furiously cycling off on their shiny mountain bikes. Their house stands out from the others as they have gleaming new windows and a new glossy black front door. Before they moved in the front garden was a riot of colourful flowers from the previous owners but they soon ripped them out, knocked down the wall and had it all concreted over so they could park their cars on it. They never notice me; I don't even warrant a second glance from them, invisible in my cloak of fatness. I did have an uneasy moment when they moved in, they looked to be about my age and I thought; what if I know them? What if I was at school with one of them? How humiliating would that be?

Then I realised that it doesn't matter, I'm not even on their radar.

Number four are renters and the tenants change every couple of years, this time around it's a middle aged man on his own so I'm guessing he's a divorcee. He scurries in and out of the front door, head down, never making eye contact. Occasionally he has a gangly, sulky looking teenage boy with him who I guess is his son. I see them coming back with McDonalds brown paper bags or white plastic carriers from Bang Thai Dee Takeaway so I presume they live on fast food whenever the son visits.

They're not fat though, even though they live on takeaways.

Numbers one and two's inhabitants are two ancient couples who must be around a hundred years old and have been here forever. Mother remembers them from when she was a child so they must be really old. The old chap at number one is always pottering around in the front garden and spends most of his time out there but I can't say the garden looks any different, I can never see that he's actually done anything. Maybe he just stays outside to keep away from his wife. There's a lot of too-ing and fro-ing at number two, lots of women in pale pink nurse type uniforms dashing in and out, early in the morning and late in the afternoon, carers, I'm guessing. They never stay for very long; twenty minutes at the most, and they always look harassed and in a hurry.

Carers, like me.

Except they get paid.

Like I said, I don't interact with the neighbours if I can possibly help it, but it's amazing what you can pick up just by watching. I do a lot of watching.

I do a quick scan of the street to make sure no one is around and then haul myself out of the car.

Time to tell Mother the good news.

'How much is it an hour?'

'£7.83' I say.

'Hmm, that's not much. Thought it would be more than that.' She frowns and the helmet of grey curls tightens.

'Minimum wage,' I say with a martyred sigh. A blatant lie, it's actually nine pounds an hour but she doesn't need to know that.

When I told her that I'd got the job – minus the blackmail details of course – she didn't seem surprised or pleased, or anything, really. What did I expect? Did I think she'd congratulate me? Say well done?

Of course not, I knew she wouldn't; but maybe a small part of me *hoped*. Hoped, that for once, I'd done something right, I'd done something on my own that she didn't feel the need to correct, belittle or condemn. I keep telling myself that I've lost all hope but I haven't; that tiny glimmer is still there and really there's nothing I can do about it because hope is involuntary, I have no control over it.

'It's because I've no experience, you know, not ever having had a job. It's not really worth it, is it Mother?' I put on a sad face as if I really don't want the job; this will ensure that she insists on me doing it. Reverse psychology, I think they call it. Mother thinks she's so clever and I'm so dim. I'm not Einstein but I'm sure I wouldn't fall for it, but she does, every single time. Luckily. She really thinks I'm too thick to be deceitful or manipulative.

'Of course it's worth it! What a ridiculous thing to say. Even if you only do two hours a day that's still £75 a week, which means I can stop paying you pocket money.'

'Okay.' I was expecting her to say this because she's so tight she almost squeaks.

'And,' she goes on, 'as you'll be so much better off you can start paying keep. Twenty pounds a week sounds fair to me, what do you think? It's about time you started contributing towards the bills. Money doesn't grow on trees you know.'

What can I say? I'll still have to look after her and do everything for her but as far as she's concerned I should do it for nothing and be grateful that I can live here so cheaply. And at the end of it all I'll only be a bit better off but I'll have to go out and work as well.

'Sounds fine, Mother.'

'Good. That's settled then.' She picks her discarded newspaper back up from the bedspread. 'I was going to have to stop your pocket money soon anyway, because I just can't afford it anymore, what with everything going up so much.'

I gawp at her and try to keep the disbelief from showing on my face; I *know* how much money she has.

'And as for the twenty pounds keep, we'll have to see how it goes. If the bills keep on going up we may have to review that, put it up a bit.' She shakes the paper to straighten out the creases then frowns at me over the top of her glasses, 'Now, are you getting me that cup of tea or not?'

'I'll get it now.' I come out of her room, down the stairs and into the kitchen before I let go of the deep breath that I'm holding. Holding my breath is one of my coping mechanisms; if I'm holding my breath I can't speak, can I? That's how I stop myself shouting at Mother. Another of my coping mechanisms is digging my toes into the floor (as long as I have shoes or slippers on). I used to clench my fists but that's too visible, she can see me doing it. So now it's the toes and the breath holding. No one can see that. The other thing with clenching my fists was fighting the urge to punch Mother, what with my hands already being in the right position.

I know that Mother won't be happy until she has every penny of my wages off me. In a few weeks' time I'll be going to work and handing every penny over to her. I think I knew this anyway but there's always that little sprig of hope that I can't control. No matter how well I know Mother there's always that little part of me that hopes that one day she'll do something nice for me, even though I know she won't. I try not to hope, but it's difficult, it's like trying to tell yourself that you're not hungry when you know you are.

Maybe if my father had stuck around things would be different; *I* would be different. Was it me that drove him away? That's what Mother says; as soon as he knew I was on the way he left, she says.

I don't even have a *photograph* of him. Only a name. And a common name at that. Even so, I could find him, I suppose, I could track him down and I have

43

thought about it, many times. I've even got as far as typing his name into Google but then I've stopped myself; why bother? He obviously has no interest in me or else he'd have made contact with me. I find it hard to believe that Mother even had a man *and* she was forty-five when I was born, so she was hardly young and pretty. I've seen the photograph album; there are some photos of her when she was younger than me and she looked middle aged and miserable then. For a while I decided that she must have been raped and that's why she dislikes me so much but then I realised that she'd tell me if she had – and enjoy telling me too.

My father must have been desperate; why else would he have been with Mother? Maybe he was jumbo sized like me and she was all he could get. Mother's such a liar too; on the rare occasions when she does answer my questions about him the story changes all of the time. On various occasions she's told me that he was a doctor, a teacher and an insurance salesman.

She has an old fashioned, heavy oak dressing table in her room and the top drawer is kept locked. I'm sure there must be something in there about my father but I've never been able to get hold of the key and I've tried, believe me.

A feeling of hopelessness washes over me.

I pick up the kettle and shove it under the tap and fill it up, then plug it onto boil. I take her china teacup and saucer out of the cupboard and put it on the tray along with two digestives on a matching plate. I'm cramming a biscuit into my mouth before I realise what I'm doing.

I taste the sweet sugary taste and it's heavenly but somehow, I manage to stop myself from biting into it. No. I am not doing this anymore.

I open the pedal bin and spit the biscuit into it.

I start to jog on the spot.

I will not give in.

She won't make me.

Chapter 5

Monday morning has arrived at last and I park my car in the free car park at the back of the library and embark the twenty-minute walk into town.

Incredible though it is I am actually choosing to walk instead of parking in the precinct car park which is only a spit away from Moppers. I have my new trainers on, freshly purchased from Foodco, black leggings and black baggy t-shirt. Veronica informed me that I will be supplied with a uniform in the Moppers corporate colours. As she never asked for my size I've deduced that it's probably going to be an apron and I wonder if it will fit around what passes for my waist.

I don't exactly march along but I don't do my normal head down shuffle; I put my head up and look straight ahead and swing my arms to build the momentum to propel me along. The jogging on the spot has definitely made a difference and even though it's only been a week I feel as if my body is responding to the exercise. I don't get so out of breath and can jog for a little longer every day without feeling as if I'm going to die.

And joy of joy, I got on the scales this morning and I've lost eight pounds.

Eight pounds in one week.

I know I won't lose so much the second week but

if I cut down a bit more then I'll lose it quicker. I haven't had breakfast this morning and I can feel the hunger gnawing in my stomach but I welcome that feeling because it means I'm losing weight.

I turn into the street where Moppers is located, marvelling at the fact that I'm out of breath but not doubled over gasping for air. Soon I'll start running outside, I'll go in the evenings when it's dark, when Mother's in bed and there'll be no one around to see or hear me thumping along the streets.

I arrive at Moppers and put my hand on the door and push; the door doesn't move. I look at my watch; eight forty-five, I'm early.

I peer through the window and through the murk I can just make out Moira sitting at her desk, engrossed in her knitting. I tap on the glass and she looks up and when she sees me she doesn't look pleased. She very slowly gets out of her seat and comes over and takes her time unlocking the door.

'The office doesn't open until nine.' She opens it a few inches, standing in front of it so that I can't get through. 'Veronica's not here yet either.'

'Okay, I'll stand outside here and stare at the wall, shall I?' I spit sarcastically. Where did that come from? Honestly, my mouth seems to have a mind of its own lately.

'There's no need to be facetious, I'm sure.' She purses her lips and reluctantly stands aside to let me in. I hear a muffled snigger from behind me and I turn and see the blonde from the interview follow behind me.

Moira returns to her desk and picks up her knitting and the blonde and I stand and look at each other.

47

'Hi,' I say, 'I'm Alison.'

'Hiya Alison, nice to meet you, I'm Doris.'

Doris? Really? Her name doesn't match her looks at all.

She waves her hand and laughs loudly. 'I know. I don't mind if you want to laugh, honest. Doris. Fucking awful innit? Dunno what me mum was finking.'

Moira sniffs her disapproval without looking up from her knitting and Doris rolls her eyes at me and mouths *old bitch* while looking pointedly at Moira.

'You starting today?'

'I am,' I say. 'You too?'

'Yeah,' Doris says. 'Surprised they wanted me to start so quick, fink they were expecting more people to apply. Ronnie asked me if I knew anyone else who wanted a job.'

The door clanging open interrupts us and Veronica appears followed by a short, red-haired woman of about forty.

The red-haired woman closes the door carefully and hovers behind Veronica. There's hardly a foot between us all and I feel a bead of sweat trickle down my back. Great. That's all I need; if I don't get out of here soon I'll turn into a sweating mess. I feel like a monster next to these tiny people.

'Ah, you're here nice and early. That's good.' She beams at me and Doris and drags the red-haired woman to the front.

'This is Rita, one of our most experienced cleaners, she's going to be showing you the Moppers Homeclean procedures.'

Rita nods at us both and smiles and we smile back.

She's wearing a bright yellow tabard with Moppers Homeclean emblazoned across the front over a crisp white blouse and a pair of pale blue jeans with such sharply ironed creases that you could slice cheese with them. I pray that we're not going to go through the procedures out here. The sweat is now running down my back.

'We doing it in here Ronnie?' Doris asks. 'Cos I ain't being funny but there ain't room to swing a cat in here.'

Veronica frowns at Doris. 'No of course not, and it's Veronica, not Ronnie. We'll go through to my office and run through the relevant health and safety procedures and then Rita will take you to one of her regulars to show you how we, at Moppers, clean.'

Thank God. I unclench my toes and quietly let out the breath I was holding. Veronica marches into her office and the three of us follow meekly behind and stand in a squished line in front of her desk. Still cosy, but manageable.

Heel tapping her way importantly to a large metal filing cabinet, Veronica yanks open a drawer, pokes around for a moment then pulls out two plastic bags and brings them over to us. You can tell a lot about someone from the way they walk; Veronica's rat-a-tat-tat heel tapping walk and pursed lips tell me she has a very high opinion of herself and a pretty low one of everyone else. Much different from my own lumbering, flat footed walk which tells you all there is to know about me and my low opinion of myself. That's going to change. I too, will have a super important walk one day.

Veronica studies the labels on the bags and then

hands one to me and one to Doris.

'Your tabards. If you lose them I will have to deduct fifteen pounds from your wages for a replacement. If you decide to leave the company and don't return them we will deduct it from your final pay packet.'

I rip open the plastic and pull out the tabard. I pull it over my head and let it hang; there's no way the straps that fit around the waist will do up so it sticks out in front of me like a giant bib. Doris pulls her on and snaps the poppers together on the straps; the yellow clashes with her hair making her skin look sallow and jaundiced.

'Now you're suitably attired,' Veronica says, casting a disgusted glance in my direction. 'I'll give you a brief rundown on health and safety and Moppers Homeclean policy.' She turns her wrist and looks at her watch. 'Should only take ten minutes and then you can be on your way.'

We arrive at a grand looking house on the other side of town and Rita parks briskly and efficiently on the driveway in front of a double garage. The houses in the street are very well spaced out with big driveways between them, some are completely hidden behind tall hedges and gates and no two houses look the same. This one looks a lot newer than some of the others I can see and the front garden has been totally blocked paved in grey stone.

'I'm parking here because I know my clients and I know that they're both at work. Never presume,' Rita says as she turns to look intently at Doris and I in the back seat, 'that you can treat a client's home like your own.'

'Of course not.' I say positively.

'As if,' Doris says.

'Now, make sure that you bring your cleaning kit and anything else that you need and we'll enter the premises. Did you bring a drink with you?'

'No,' we chorus.

'Okay. Well it's acceptable to have a drink of water at a client's house as long as you wash up and put away the glass afterwards. Strictly NO helping yourself to any other beverages. Although, personally, I always bring my own.'

Here we go again. In the twenty-minute drive from Moppers, Rita hasn't drawn breath.

'Can't be too careful with my allergy. Could be fatal, you know, if a peanut were to pass my lips.'

Yes, we do know, having been told about a million times. Rita has a peanut allergy and if the merest trace of a peanut were to pass her lips she'd be jettisoned into anaphylactic shock and certain death. Her words, not mine.

'That's why I always bring my own.' She holds up a small bottle of water and gives it a little shake. 'Never take a chance, I always need to know exactly what I'm eating and drinking.' To prove a point, she unscrews the top and takes a gulp then screws the lid back on again.

I don't say anything and call me fussy but if I had an allergy as dangerous as hers I don't think I'd be swigging straight out of a bottle of water bought from Foodco, even though I can't actually think of any drinks that contain peanuts. Suppose the person stacking the shelves had a trace of peanut on their hands and it got onto the bottle? If the merest hint of peanut could prove fatal, would you take the chance? I wouldn't.

'Right! Let's go ladies and I'll show you how to clean the Moppers way.'

Doris and I scrabble out of the back seats and Rita holds the front passenger door open while we haul ourselves through the gap; not easy when you're my size. Doris gets out first and after a lot of huffing and puffing I finally emerge from the car like a cork out of a bottle while Rita and Doris avert their eyes to mask their embarrassment. For some reason I wasn't allowed to sit in the front seat, that space being reserved for all of our cleaning kits.

Rita stands at the front door and rummages around in her pocket, then produces a key and holds it up for inspection.

'The client has been good enough to allow us to hold a key to their property and it's our duty to make sure that we look after the key and not let it fall into the wrong hands. When not being used it must always be kept in a secure location within your own home.'

Doris and I stand mutely while Rita solemnly unlocks and opens the door.

'Now, before we go in I'll remind you of the procedure. Do NOT move from the doormat until you are wearing your foot covers.'

One at a time we enter the house, first Rita, then Doris, then me. In turn we stand on the doormat and cover our shoes with the paper foot covers provided by Moppers. Suitably wrapped we pick up our cleaning kits and follow Rita through to the kitchen.

'I always start in the kitchen as it usually takes the

longest,' Rita says as she puts her kit down on the floor.

'Never,' she straightens up, 'ever, put your cleaning kit on a table or any furniture in case it causes damage or scratches. Always the floor.' She taps the floor with her paper wrapped toe in case we don't understand her.

We place our kits neatly next to hers.

'We're not paid to wash up but as these are my regulars if they've left anything out I do stack the dishwasher for them and put it on.'

I look around the kitchen to see that every worktop is littered with dirty dishes; it doesn't look like they've washed up for days, in fact they could probably give me a run for my money. Well, how I used to be, not now.

'Fuck me, doesn't look like they've washed up for a week,' Doris says as she surveys the kitchen in disgust. 'They might be posh but they ain't very clean.'

'Doris! Please don't use language like that. We Moppers have a reputation to think of. And remember, our clients have busy lives and that's why they hire us. They don't have time to clean. Now, you scrape the plates and I'll stack.' She pulls open the dishwasher which is full of clean crockery and starts to unload it.

Doris and I start scraping and stacking the plates. The kitchen is lovely, like something out of a glossy magazine spread. Chunky wooden worktops with shiny cream cupboards, all smooth curved edges and brushed aluminium handles. And a dishwasher; how fantastic never having to wash up again. Just open the door and hide all of it away and when you open it later on it's all magically clean and sparkling.

Once the dishwasher is loaded Rita turns it on with a twist of a knob and starts running hot water into the sink.

'Assuming there's no washing up to be done the next job is to wipe all of the worktops, clean the cooker top – not the oven; if they want the oven cleaned that's an extra and has to be paid for, and when you've done that the floor needs to be mopped. Once I've done the rest of the house the floor will be dry by then and I'll then thoroughly clean the sink. Remembering,' she frowns at us to emphasise her point, 'to use the correct cloths at all times.'

Ah, yes, the correct cloths. We have packs of different coloured cloths; blue for the kitchen, pink for the bath and hand basin, green for the toilet and yellow for dusting. On no account are we to use the same cloth for say, toilets and sinks or God forbid, different houses. We are to wash the cloths at our own expense in our own washing machines at a wash of at least sixty degrees and will only be issued with new packets of cloths when we produce the worn-out ones they're to replace. Any infringement of these rules will result in disciplinary action although how they would know I've no idea.

When Veronica was lecturing us on the use of the cloths Doris started to laugh which she quickly turned into a cough when Veronica glared at her. On our way out to Rita's Ford Fiesta Doris put her hand in front of her mouth and whispered to me, 'I'll be using the same fucking cloth on everything. Not like it's my house. I won't be washing them neither.'

We stand and watch as Rita shows us the correct way to wipe a worktop and cooker. I stifle a yawn. I'll be glad to get this over with and get on with it; tomorrow I have my first client. I wonder if the house will be as nice as this one.

'Now,' Rita announces, 'bathrooms next! Then the bedrooms and lastly, the lounge. Then the kitchen sink and last of all, the vacuuming.'

We follow Rita's brisk little bottom up the stairs and into the main bathroom. We watch while she plunges the toilet brush down the toilet, furiously scrubbing, red curls bobbing with the effort, then the pink cloth is rubbed in fast and furious circles around the hand basin and bath. She's value for money, I'll give her that, and very quick and thorough.

I think she's enjoying showing off and I do wonder if she's normally this particular. Every so often she pulls her bottle of water from her trouser pocket and takes a tiny sip from it to remind us of her allergy.

We follow her as she flies around the bedrooms in no time at all; four bedrooms altogether with one of them being used as a study; bundles of wires spill over a desk with a laptop still open next to it. Another bedroom has a huge running machine in it and the second biggest is set up as a guest room but clearly hasn't been slept in recently.

The master bedroom is gorgeous, a walk-in wardrobe filled with clothes, his and hers rails each side with a bank of drawers in the centre. I gaze at in awe; what sort of life must these people live? How many clothes can one person wear? Just two people living in a house this size, how do some people get to be so lucky?

Doris and I stand and watch as Rita flits around the room, Doris yawns loudly and then winks at me when Rita looks at her disapprovingly.

I think Rita is bored with showing off and fed up with us watching her and, as we come downstairs, Doris is directed to clean the kitchen sink thoroughly while I'm given instructions to dust the lounge while Rita vacuums.

The lounge is minimalist but none the less stunning; glass doors the length of one side of the room open out onto the back garden which is huge; wooden decking gives way to a large expanse of grass which is bordered by trees. I've no doubt that these people have a gardener too. In front of the glass doors sits a chrome and glass dining table with eight chairs arranged around it. The chairs are made of chrome and beige leather and are almost deck chair like in design. A massive cream sideboard sits alongside and I wonder what it's made of to have such a glossy shine.

Two cream velvety sofas face each other across a vast glass topped coffee table, the sister to the dining table, glossy magazines scattered over the top. An enormous television dominates the wall opposite the doors; I can't imagine these people watching normal programmes like me, certainly not soaps and reality tv. I expect they watch the news and documentaries and arty films.

I begin to dust; I sweep my yellow duster over the coffee table and arrange the magazines into a tidy pile. I carefully trail my duster over the television screen, afraid to press too hard in case I damage it. I pick up the sumptuous cushions from the sofa; velvety and plump I hold them to my nose and inhale; they smell sweet and flowery. I plump them and arrange them symmetrically on the sofa and stand back and admire them and then do the same to the other sofa. It's such a lovely house I can see why Rita takes such a pride in making it look clean and pristine.

I spray the table and polish it, making sure to get every smear out of it so I can see my reflection. I stand back and admire my handiwork and feel ridiculously pleased with myself. I run the cloth up and down the chrome legs on the chairs and table making sure there are no smears.

There. Perfect.

'My word, you've done a good job and so quickly too.'

Rita is standing in the doorway with her hands on her hips watching me.

'Just the sideboard to do and that's it,' I say, thrilled. A good job, she said I'd done a good job. I realise that I can't remember the last time I received a compliment.

'Well done, Alison, keep it up.' She turns and goes back into the hall.

I turn to the sideboard and pick up a picture frame to dust with a huge smile on my face. I run the duster around the frame and over the photograph of the couple with film star looks smiling back at me; he has dark hair and twinkly blue eyes, perfect teeth and a deep tan. She is blonde and beautiful, every man's dream girl; the perfect couple who live in this perfect house.

And then I realise that it's fate; serendipity,

whatever you want to call it.

Because the girl in the photograph is Bella.

Chapter 6

I close the front door quietly and jog down the path using my mini torch to guide me. The evening is cold but is it slightly warmer than last week, is that the tiniest hint of spring in the night air? It's getting near the end of March so I'm hopeful.

I jog along Duck Pond Lane and head towards The Rise. I've come to enjoy my nightly runs; at first I could barely make it to the end of the street without getting out of breath. My body felt as if it didn't belong to me and I had no control over it; great wobbling chunks of fat bouncing up and down as I thundered along. But I'm getting used to it now and I'm running further every night and the blubbery bits definitely feel smaller.

I use these late night runs to think and plan my future; to shake off the stress of caring for Mother and being at her beck and call. I fantasise about a life where I can do as I please and people look at me with admiration, not disgust.

I run past The Rise pointing my torch in front to guide me as there are no street lights here. There's no light pollution at all but the pitch blackness doesn't bother me even though last year a serial killer buried one of his victims here. I have no fear. I feel sure I could out run an attacker or failing that, squash one.

I'm transforming; slowly but surely. What started out as jogging on the spot has developed into nightly runs that are getting longer and longer; last night I ran for over an hour and I didn't want to go back home even though the muscles in my legs were burning and screaming for a rest. I wanted to run as far away from Mother as possible; if only I had somewhere else to go then I'd never go back. In the last month I've had a taste of normal life and I love it. I clean for my regular clients for two hours every day and even though most of them are out when I clean I feel I've come to know them. Mrs Forsyth; Mondays and Fridays - so she's all ready for the weekend on a Friday and the weekend clean up on a Monday, she says. On the first day I arrived the house was spotless, I asked her where she wanted me to start and she said *let's have a cup of tea first, shall we?* And we sat there for two hours and she told me all about her son in Scotland and her daughter who does something very important (although I can't remember what) in London. Mrs Forsyth says that they have very busy lives and it doesn't sound as if she sees them very much. But she sounds so proud of them; I wish I had a mother like her. She talks about her late husband, Mr Forsyth she calls him, a lot. They travelled all over the world because he worked for a massive company who were always posting him to different places. I quickly realised that she's lonely and doesn't need a cleaner at all and that the weekends loom long and lonely for her. She just wants someone to talk to. And I'm quite happy to talk to her; she's a lovely old lady and has had a very interesting life but I do feel a bit bad that I'm getting paid for doing nothing. I did say that to her and she said, *my dear, don't you worry about that. I can afford it and I like your company so we'll say no more about it.* I haven't told Moppers for obvious reasons and Mrs Forsyth is a new customer so no one has cleaned for her before so it's our little secret.

Mr Pascoe's another of mine; he's a professor of something at Bristol University and he lives mainly on tinned Fray Bentos pies and tinned new potatoes. I've never met him but you can tell a lot by the contents of rubbish bins. His furniture is dark, heavy, old and knocked about but looks as if it was once very expensive and came from a much grander house than his three-bed semi. His wardrobe is full of brown and beige trousers, checked shirts in brushed cotton and thick, bobbly jumpers that smell slightly of mothballs. I feel sure I'd know him if I saw him.

I run out of The Rise and past The George pub and along the terraced streets. I zig zag up and down all of these streets and sometimes people leave their curtains open and I can see right in. I don't even feel nosy because if they didn't want people looking they'd close their curtains, wouldn't they? The blue flickering light of a television, small children playing when they should be fast asleep, a family party. Once, a young couple having a huge row, standing in front of their television shouting at each other with red, angry faces. One night I saw a house party in full swing, the front door thrown wide open even though it was freezing. The thump of music and laughter washed over me as I ran by and I suddenly felt so alone, so friendless. A man was standing on the doorstep smoking and I expected an insult as I pounded by but he shouted, *hey love, give that up and come in and have a drink.*

I've lost over two and a half stone now; I can see and feel the changes, I've become reacquainted with the sight of my feet. Oh, I still have a long way to go but I know I can do it. As well as the running I've bought myself some weights to tone up and I'm sure I can feel the teeniest hint of muscle in my arms.

Mother hasn't noticed of course and I don't want her to, she wouldn't like it, she doesn't like change. It would frighten her, the thought of me losing weight; as if her hold over me would disappear along with the pounds. I'm still wearing the same clothes, the same leggings which are baggier now and the same t-shirts that hang looser. I don't want to buy any new clothes until I'm slim and I can put them on and revel in how good I look.

My job as a cleaner is hardly a career but I like it, I like getting away from Mother and seeing other people. It's been such a long time that I've socialised with anyone; that I've actually felt able to interact with anyone else without feeling that I should apologise for even existing. I *like* talking to people.

I only have to go into the Moppers office once a week, on Fridays, to take in my time sheets but I make an effort to talk to the other cleaners instead of standing mute and trying to be invisible and each time it gets easier, less of an effort and more of a pleasure. Rita, the redhead, is always pleasant but holds herself as being superior to the rest of us as she's been there the longest. I did ask her if she wanted to swap Bella for one of my clients; I was even prepared to give her Mrs Forsyth – although I would have felt a bit guilty about it – but I didn't get as far as offering as it was an emphatic *no*. She looked at me a bit strangely and asked why would I even want to do that? I said I had a friend who lived over near them so I'd be able to combine the clean with a visit. I'm not sure she believed me and I felt myself starting to blush.

There's a couple of youngsters who clean, they fit it around their college hours and they started at the same time as me but apparently the students never last long as it's too much like hard work, according to Rita. Then there are a couple of retired ladies who do it to supplement their pensions, crimplened and twin-setted they always look far too smart to get their hands dirty. Their hair always looks freshly washed and set and they always have lipstick on too.

Doris the blonde and I have become quite friendly. The first Friday after I handed my time sheet in I came out of the door and she was standing in front of the shop window smoking a cigarette so I stopped to ask her how she was getting on. We talked for so long that we ended up going to Joey's Café for a cup of tea and now we do it every week. Mother asked why I was so long and I told her that we have a weekly update meeting about health and safety. She'd only make it her mission to spoil it if she knew I had a friend; she wouldn't be able to stand it. She's not happy about the mythical health and safety meeting though; says it's not right and that I should get paid for it.

So I can give it all to her.

True to form, I'd only been at Moppers for two weeks when she put my rent up to thirty pounds a week. She used the latest electricity bill as the excuse, said it had gone up astronomically and she'd struggle to pay it. All lies of course but what can I do? No doubt the next bill that comes in will be the excuse to put it up again.

Doris thinks I'm really lucky – I haven't been completely truthful about Mother. I haven't exactly lied, I just haven't told her what Mother's really like. She says she'd give her eye teeth to be in my position – the run of a big house and minimal rent. She imagines Mother as a sweet little old lady confined to her room who just has to be fed now and again. I don't disillusion her; Doris is the first friend I've had for a very long time and I don't want our friendship to be all about *Mother*.

Doris lives with her boyfriend, Charlie. To quote Doris, *he's a hot shag but a bit of a wanker*. He never has a job for very long and is always getting 'laid off' which I think means he gets the sack. She says it's because he won't get out of bed in the morning. He gets the sack, gets a new job, makes an effort for a few weeks, then starts missing days and gets the sack again. She grumbles about him but I think she loves him or else she wouldn't put up with him, would she?

She asked me if I had a boyfriend! I was flattered – as if anyone would look at me. And do you know what I did? I lied. I didn't say I had a boyfriend now but I pretended I used to have one. I even gave him a name, Bruce; don't even ask where that came from. My only excuse is I was thinking on the hoof, so to speak, and actually I do know where it came from; I'd been cleaning at Mrs Forsyth's and I thought Bruce, that'll do. Doris did ask me if he was Australian and I told her no, but his mum was.

I sort of surprised myself with how easily I lied; with a bit of forethought and planning I could be quite good at it.

Which will be useful when I start my new life as the new me because there's no way I'll be advertising the fact that I used to be a gigantic loser.

I've pounded along the same streets four times now so I stop under a streetlamp and look at my watch, 11:35 I've been running for an hour and twenty minutes. My legs are tired and I can feel the sweat dripping down my back but I feel so good; so alive.

I reluctantly head back in the direction of The Rise towards home. If I stay out any longer I won't be able to drag myself out of bed in the morning. Running is becoming an obsession, if it wasn't for Mother I could run all night. It's just coming up to midnight as I unlock the front door and let myself in. I close it gently and quietly lock it.

'ALISON!'

Mother's shriek makes me jump, she's normally fast asleep from around nine in the evening until at least eight o'clock the next morning.

'Alison! Are you there? Have you just come in?'

I quietly slip my feet out of my trainers and tiptoe into the lounge. I pick up the throw from the back of the sofa and wrap it around myself then pull my hair out of its pony tail and mess it up.

'Mother?' I call feebly trying to make my voice sound as if I've just woken up.

'Are you coming upstairs or do I have to shout all night?'

I climb the stairs, frantically trying to calm my breathing. I open the door to Mother's room to be greeted by the sight of her sitting up in bed with her bedside lamp on.

'I've been calling you for ages, where have you been?' She looks at me accusingly.

'Fell asleep, Mother.'

'Why didn't you hear me? I could have died up here.'

Oh God. I hope this isn't going to develop into one of her episodes; we're overdue for one.

I walk over to the bed and start smoothing the bedclothes and tucking her in.

'Get off me!' she bats my hands away, 'I've got one of my heads and I need to take my pills and YOU never left me a glass of water.'

I look at the bedside table; she's right, no glass of water. A stupid mistake which I seem to be making more of lately.

'Sorry,' I say sweetly, 'I'll get you one straight away.'

I dash downstairs and run her a glass of water then rush back upstairs and present it to her.

She takes it without comment and I undo her bottle of painkillers and hand her two. She swallows them and takes a long drink of water and then hands the glass back to me.

'Have you been out?'

'Of course not, Mother. Where would I go?'

I can see the struggle on her face; she doesn't believe me. She thinks I've been out but the rational part of her knows that I have no friends and nowhere to go.

'You've not been seeing men, have you?'

I laugh; a genuine laugh because I can't believe she could even think that.

'Of course not, Mother, whatever gives you that idea.'

'I thought I heard the front door. You haven't had anyone down there, have you? You know I don't like people coming into my house.'

'Of course no one else was down there! I think I maybe had the TV on too loud so I didn't hear you.'

She studies my face and I try not to squirm; she's done this ever since I was a child and has an uncanny knack of knowing when I'm lying, when I'm trying to hide something. Despite my developing lying skills with other people it's still hard to fool Mother.

'You've changed,' she states flatly, and I wonder if she's noticed the weight loss. 'Ever since you took that cleaning job, you've not been the same.'

'I haven't changed, Mother, I'm just the same,' I say. 'Shall I plump your pillows up for you?'

She doesn't answer but moves forward and I plump the pillows and she settles back and I tuck the coverlet around her. Her mouth is set in a grim line and she doesn't take her eyes off me.

'Is that okay, Mother?'

She says nothing but looks at me suspiciously and I make a mental note to be more careful.

'Sleep well, Mother.' I turn out her bedside light. 'I'll see you in the morning.'

She doesn't answer and I'm in the doorway when she speaks.

'First thing tomorrow I want you to ring that stair lift man, the one that gave us the quote. I need to be able to get downstairs.'

I turn around and look at her, struggling to keep the horror from showing on my face.

67

'And don't be thinking you can put me off because you can't.'

I open my mouth like a gaping goldfish but nothing comes out.

'Because,' Mother pulls herself up on her elbows, 'I don't trust you my girl, you're up to something and I need to get downstairs so I can keep an eye on you.'

Oh no.

No, no, no, no, no.

Chapter 7

It's not nice to profit by misfortune but I can't say that I'm not glad that Rita has rung in sick. Veronica asked if anyone would like to do extra shifts for a few weeks, possibly longer, and I shot my hand up in the air and shouted 'Me please' before anyone beat me to it. I felt a bit foolish as soon as I'd done it because everyone looked at me as if I were a proper idiot – putting my hand up like that as if I was still at school. Anyway, I'm not going to worry about that because I got an extra shift and I'm going to be cleaning Bella's house. I said I could do a Monday if that was any use as I knew that was the day for Bella's clean, I can fit it around Mrs Forsyth's. The two twin set ladies took the rest of her shifts but they didn't put their hands up like a couple of school kids, they had to be cajoled into it as no one else was really interested.

I'm so excited, it feels like it's meant to be.

I sort of knew it was going to happen, strange though it sounds. It was just a matter of time.

I know it must sound trivial and a bit weird, but knowing that I'm going to be cleaning Bella's house makes me feel closer to her. I already feel like she's done so much for me even though she doesn't know it – if I hadn't seen her that day then I wouldn't be where I am now. I'd still be stuffing my face and getting fatter and fatter; I wouldn't have even thought about getting a job and I wouldn't have a *plan*.

I had a bad night last night though, I couldn't sleep for thinking about that bloody stair lift. The thought of Mother being able to get downstairs is unbearable and it simply *cannot* happen. I won't be able to do a thing if she's downstairs with me; I'd have to hide my laptop away, I'd never be able to watch anything that I want on television again and as for running – she'll never allow it. I'd be banned from leaving the house completely and made to sit with her and watch quiz shows all night. And then there's the garden; she's under the illusion that I maintain it. The thought of her reaction to seeing the garden is enough to drive me straight to the biscuit tin. I'm fitter now and I probably could get out there and wrestle it back into some sort of shape but that would impact on my running.

And anyway, I don't want to.

And what if she gets it into her head that if she can get downstairs she can get in the car and I can take her shopping with me? Visions of me pushing her around Foodco in a wheelchair while she regally chooses the food kept me awake for hours; no more microwave meals.

Oh God, the microwave, that'll have to go too.

My life will be *hell*.

No. It simply cannot happen. I'm going to stall her for now, at least all of those sleepless hours were useful for formulating a plan of sorts. I'm going to pretend to Mother that I've already made a phone call to the stair lift people. I'll tell her that as it was over three months ago since they measured up they have to do a fresh quote and the earliest they can come to do it is two weeks' time. She won't like it one little bit and I'll just have to hope she doesn't decide to phone them herself.

Maybe the telephone extension in her room will develop a fault, which might be a good idea anyway as I'm never too sure whether she's listening in or not. I'll have to wait until she's in the bath and do something to it, disable it somehow.

'We going for a coffee, Al?'

'What?'

'Coffee? You alright? Everyfing alright?' Doris is looking at me with concern.

I laugh, 'Yeah, course it is, sorry, I was miles away.'

Moppers tiny office empties rapidly, time sheets deposited and wage queries dealt with. I tuck the sheet of paper, with Bella's address and cleaning hours that Veronica has given me, into my bag. I don't need the address; I've driven around there many times on my way back from Foodco. I'm not stalking her or anything weird like that, I just like to look at the house, imagine how fabulous her life is.

Imagine if my life were like hers.

Doris and I come out of Moppers and wander down to Joey's Café. It's my turn to get the drinks and I go up to the counter while Doris bags the table by the window.

I pay for the teas and take them over to the table and put them down, careful not to spill them, then slide into the seat opposite Doris. She watches me with a thoughtful expression as I sit down.

'Penny for them?' I say.

Doris heaps three spoonsful of sugar into her tea and stirs it.

'I was watching you as you brought the teas over.'

'Were you?'

'Yeah I was. I can see a big difference in you – how much have you lost now?'

'Getting on for three stone.' I can't help the big smile on my face, 'probably got another four to go.' Nearly halfway there.

'You should market your diet, I've never seen anyone lose it so quick.'

'Starving myself and running until I drop – don't think it'd be that popular, most people want to lose weight without doing any exercise or eating less.'

'You've done it though.'

'True. But it's taken me a long time to realise that I could only do it if I changed my whole attitude and stopped stuffing.'

Doris laughs, 'So who's the lucky bloke then? You've got to be doing this for a bloke, innit? Otherwise why would you be bovvering?'

'No, there's no bloke, honest.'

'Liar, there's always a bloke behind it.' She leans forward. 'Or are you getting ready to meet someone, a new you sort of fing?'

'Maybe.' I shrug. 'But I've a way to go yet.' Bella's my secret; Doris wouldn't understand how Bella has changed my life, changed the way I think. It's all black and white to Doris, she'd probably think I'm a lesbian and even if I could convince her I wasn't she'd definitely think I was a complete weirdo or a stalker.

'You'll get there,' Doris says confidently, 'cos you're determined, I can see it, you're, what's the word?'

I shake my head, 'I don't know.'

'Motivated!' she sits back, pleased with herself, 'That's the word, motivated.'

Maybe I am.

'Two weeks! Why do they need to come back and re-measure? The house hasn't changed, the stairs haven't changed, I've never heard such complete nonsense.'

'That's exactly what I said to them but they're insisting on a new survey.'

'Ridiculous, I've a good mind to ring them and give them a piece of my mind.'

I thought she might say that so I've taken the precaution of leaving the phone off the hook downstairs. Just in case.

'Good idea,' I say in a positive tone, 'Shall I help you have your shower first? You've plenty of time, they don't close until five.'

She ponders this for a while; she usually likes to have her shower at around ten o'clock in the morning but we've had to change this to accommodate my cleaning job. She's not happy about it but as I've told her I can't pick and choose when I clean other peoples' houses. Actually, I can, but she doesn't know that.

She harrumphs and looks at the clock as if it's going to tell her what to do. It's nearly lunchtime because of my Friday catch up with Doris.

'Okay. I'll have my shower first otherwise it'll be bedtime and then there'll be no point in bothering.' I can't see what difference it makes; she goes straight back to bed afterwards, it's not as if she gets dressed, she just puts a clean nightie on.

'Okay, you have your shower and after that I'll make some lunch.' I go into her en-suite, turn on the shower and make sure the pull-down seat is ready underneath it.

'Not too hot, mind,' she bellows at me. As if I need telling.

While the shower is running I push her walker up to the side of the bed and help her up and hold the walker still while she positions herself in front of it. She pushes my hands away as I try to guide her towards the bathroom.

'I don't need you to help me! I've been managing to get to the toilet on my own while you've been out gallivanting.'

Gallivanting. Yes. In Mother's world cleaning other people's houses is gallivanting.

'Once that stair lift is installed I'll be a lot more independent.' She shuffles into the bathroom and stops in the doorway and turns her head around and looks at me.

'You're not indispensable you know, I can manage perfectly well without you.' With that she shuffles two more steps and shuts the bathroom door with a bang and I'm left alone in her room.

I stand for a moment staring at the closed door. Why does she hate me so much? What have I ever done to make her so dislike me? I try my best, looking after her.

Well, apart from the microwave meals and looking at her bank account, but that's not so bad, is it? I try to be cheerful and do it with a smile on my face but maybe she can see straight through me and knows I resent her.

I give myself a mental shake. Get on with it. I don't have very long.

I pad quietly to the bathroom and place my ear against the door and listen; I hear the splash of the shower as Mother washes herself. She doesn't hang about; wash, rinse and out, that's Mother. I tiptoe quickly across the room and rummage around in her bedside cabinet drawer, pushing pill bottles and assorted herbal remedies aside until I find the nail scissors. I trace the lead coming out of the phone down the back of the cabinet to the extension socket behind. Pulling the cabinet away from the wall I stretch the lead to the front and near to the floor, out of sight, I make a small nick in the cable. Unnoticeable unless you look for it and there's no way Mother going to get down there. I quietly pick up the receiver and listen. Silence, no dialling tone. Mission accomplished. I silently replace the receiver.

'Open the door!' Mother bellows from the bathroom.

I push the cabinet back into place and get up and walk across to the en-suite.

'Hurry up will you!'

Needs me now, doesn't she?

I let myself out of the front door and jog down the path. I feel the tension slowly leave my shoulders as I start to run. I've waited until ten thirty to come out to make sure that Mother is definitely asleep. To say I'd had enough of her for one day is a complete understatement; totally unreasonable, argumentative and downright nasty describes Mother today.

Every day, actually.

When she discovered that the phone wasn't working she was so incensed that I thought she was going to have another stroke. She went *mad;* shouting, screaming, demanding that I call a telephone engineer out *immediately* and get it fixed *right now.* I told her it wasn't that simple and that it would take a few days but she just kept on and on and in the end, I went downstairs and stood in the lounge for a while and then went back up and told her that the phone downstairs wasn't working either.

'Use your mobile and report it.' She bellowed at me. I hadn't even thought of that; there's me thinking I could just cut her phone off and she'd put up with it. How stupid was that?

As if.

I stood in front of her and I just couldn't *think*, I felt in a complete panic. And then a crafty look came over her face and she demanded that I get my mobile phone and bring it upstairs and she would *do it herself.* I trotted back downstairs like a half-wit and went into the lounge and sat on the sofa shaking while I racked my brains to think of an excuse. Honestly, I felt like crying. She started shouting for me again so I went back upstairs and told her I couldn't find my phone and I must have left it at Moppers this morning. This caused more screaming and I could tell she didn't believe me which isn't surprising as it was pretty feeble.

So much for my stupid plan; I thought I was being so clever but I've only made things worse and I don't know how I'm going to sort this mess out. I'll have to get a telephone engineer to come out and fix her phone and I'll have to arrange for that oily stair lift salesman to come out, too. Because she's determined to have a stair lift this time, come what may. She's got it into her head that I'm up to something, which I am, and she thinks that once she's downstairs I won't be able to do anything without her knowing.

I may as well just give up the running and turn around and go back home and eat and eat until I explode.

I don't though, the jog gradually turns into a run, faster and faster as if the increasing speed will cause a solution to magically present itself to me. I pound past The Rise and speed up even more; it's going to be a long run tonight, I need to try and think of *something*.

I run and run, zig-zagging across the same streets with the same thoughts spinning through my mind on a loop; how to stop Mother getting the stair lift and ruining my life.

I run for two hours and my calf muscles are starting to cramp and my lungs feel as if they're going to burst.

There is no solution.

I change direction and head back towards home with a heavy heart and my eyes smart and sting and I realise I'm crying.

There's nothing to be done.

I've thought and thought and I can't think of a way to stop her. One simple obstacle and I can't think of a way out. A familiar feeling of disgust with myself overwhelms me and my plans for a bright, shiny new life seem fantastic and impossible. Why did I even think that I could change my life with the millstone of Mother around my neck? Who did I think I was fooling?

As I turn into Duck Pond Lane I see the familiar cold, stone outline of our house and from nowhere the solution hits me, so shockingly that I stumble and nearly fall, only my outstretched hands prevent a full face plant into the road. I pick myself up and dust the gravel from my palms and stare at Mother's bedroom window in wonder. The answer is so simple and blindingly obvious that I can't understand why I didn't think of it before. How could I not have seen it?

The answer was there all of the time staring me in the face; all it requires is for me to grow a backbone and stand up to Mother, start defending myself.

I've said it myself; without a stair lift Mother is helpless; she can get out of bed and shuffle to the bathroom on her own but she very rarely does in spite of all she says. Mostly she waits for me to help her because she's terrified of falling and hurting herself, her morbid fear of breaking bones and being taken to hospital and dying there prevents her.

Mother has dominated me for so long that I haven't been able to see that without my help she cannot function; I do everything for her. She spends her life ordering me around but what can she actually do if I choose to ignore her commands?

Nothing.

She can shout at me, belittle me, threaten me, but what can she actually do?

Absolutely nothing.

Without me she'd be helpless, she'd need carers to come in and look after her and how's she going to get them unless I organise them for her? Her telephone doesn't work and short of banging on her window to attract attention from any passers-by, which are few and far between, who's going to know she's up there? She doesn't have any friends, anyone to care about her, except me. She's made sure to isolate herself and me from anyone else. She could be dead and no one would know.

She thinks she holds the purse strings but she doesn't really; if I wanted to I could take control of her bank account and empty it. I have access to it and I already use her bank card. She can't hurt me, she can threaten to throw me out but how can she do that if she can't leave her room?

A giggle escapes me and I start to laugh and I wonder if I might be mad; nearly one o'clock in the morning and I'm standing in the street laughing until the tears roll down my face and my ribs ache.

I've been such a blind, downtrodden fool.

The answer's been there the whole time.

I'm the one with the power.

Chapter 8

'You seem very chipper today, dear, have you been up to something nice at the weekend?' Mrs Forsyth sets my cup of tea on the table and sits down opposite me. She's such a love, she won't even let me make a cup of tea for her, let alone do the cleaning that I get paid for.

'Oh, nothing special. Took Mother out for a drive in the countryside for a change of scenery but nothing much apart from that.' I amaze myself at how easily the lie trips off my tongue.

'You're so good to your mother, she must be so proud of you.'

I say nothing but smile and take a sip of tea.

'Cake, dear?' Mrs Forsyth proffers a plate of daintily sliced Battenburg.

I shake my head, 'Not for me thank you, although it looks delicious.'

'Oh, silly me.' Mrs Forsyth slaps herself on the wrist. 'I mustn't tempt you, you're doing so well. They'll soon be nothing of you at the rate you're going.'

I thought that the weight loss would slow down but if anything it's speeded up; the longer my nocturnal runs get the more weight I lose. I've had to buy another pair of trainers from Foodco because the ones I bought when I started running are too big –

they actually flop off my feet; I've gone down two shoe sizes. My feet look almost normal now and hardly bulge over the top of ballet flats at all.

'Did I ever tell you the story about Mr Forsyth and the time we were posted to Singapore?'

'No,' I say, lying again. 'That must have been quite exciting, what was Singapore like?'

I fix an interested expression on my face as Mrs Forsyth happily tells me a story I've heard many times before. I did listen the first time so I don't feel too bad and I'm getting quite adept at making the appropriate noises in the right places.

I zone out and ponder the events of the last couple of days. The weekend started like any other; Mother demanding this, that and the other; cooking, cleaning and running up and down the stairs to her. Her soup was too hot, the bread was dry, the towels were hard because I used the wrong fabric conditioner, the vacuum too noisy, the tea too weak, the toast not buttered enough.

A Saturday like any other.

And I behaved like I always have done; apologising, cajoling, tip toeing around her so as not to spark one of her episodes.

I think, maybe, in my own mind, I was giving her one last chance to change; to be nicer, to be more reasonable, before I told her how it was going to be from now on.

The shock on her face was a picture.

And she didn't believe me; she thought she could shout and scream and bully and threaten me to get her own way, just as she's always done.

It started with the telephone; I wondered how long

it would take her to realise that it still wasn't working. Longer than I thought as it turned out. It took her until lunchtime so I think it must have slipped her mind and it wasn't until I took her lunch in–scrambled eggs on toast and a cup of tea –that she remembered because as I walked into the room she had the receiver in her hand.

'The telephone still isn't working,' she said mulishly, holding it aloft. 'Bring me up your mobile. I want to make a call to the stair lift people.'

'I shouldn't think they work Saturdays,' I said in my most pleasant voice.

'I'll try them anyway. Get me your mobile. I'll keep it until the engineers come and fix the phone.'

'They're not coming.'

'What?' she has that edge to her voice, the edge that will soon turn into a screech. 'Haven't you called them? I thought you were going to pick your phone up this morning when you went shopping.'

'No. I didn't. It was downstairs all of the time but I didn't want you to use it. And there's nothing wrong with the landline, the one downstairs works perfectly well.'

She looks momentarily confused and amazingly is quiet for a moment, but not for long. The calm before the storm.

'MINE doesn't work.' She waves the phone around.

'Oh, that.' I pulled the legs out on the tray and placed it carefully over her lap. 'That'll be because I cut the cable.'

Her mouth made a perfect O of surprise, a bit like a fish just landed in the net, gasping for air. An old, miserable trout.

'WHAT are you talking about?'

'I cut it,' I said in my most reasonable tone, 'with your nail scissors. So you can't use it.'

Puzzlement quickly gave way to anger which is Mother's default for everything.

'You had better explain yourself, my girl. And quickly.'

'Okay,' I said, settling myself down on the foot of her bed, 'but eat your scrambled egg before it gets cold, because that's something that's going to change around here – eat what you're given or go without. No more cooking something else because you don't like what's on offer.'

She never did eat that scrambled egg, or the toast, or even drink her tea.

She had one of her episodes, of course, I wouldn't have expected anything less. I told her that there'd be no stair lift and no telephone but things could go on pretty much as they always had. I'd still look after her, cook her meals, clean, shop; everything I'd always done. Nothing would change as far as she was concerned except that I would be doing what I wanted from now on and I wouldn't be kowtowing to her and putting up with her nonsense anymore.

She didn't believe me of course, she thinks I don't have the guts so she started with her shouting and nastiness and do you know what I did? I left. I closed her door, quietly, went downstairs and put my trainers on and went out for a nice long run for a couple of hours. It was nice to run in daylight and I didn't feel embarrassed at all because although I'm not slim I'm not supersized anymore, I'm normal fat-but-is-running-to-lose-weight size, and no one gave me a second glance.

When I came back I wondered if she'd still be shouting but the house was quiet when I let myself in. I ran up the stairs and opened her door and she was still awake – I thought she might have worn herself out and gone to sleep – still sitting there with the tray on her lap with her lunch gone cold.

I walked over and picked the tray up, and all the while she watched me with plain hatred on her face.

'Are you sure you don't want this Mother? I asked pleasantly, 'Dinner's not for another couple of hours.'

Her look of rage was comical and I had to swallow down a giggle. Because it is funny and I don't know why it's taken me so long to see it; all this time I've been the one with the power and I've let her boss me around and make my life hell. I think it's because I'm the nicer person; nicer than her. I'll still be nice, in my way, but I won't be ordered around anymore. Anyway, she opened her mouth, probably to shout at me, but before she could speak I held up my index finger and waved it at her.

'Just to remind you Mother, of our previous conversation. If you want me to do anything for you then you need to be civil to me, you need to speak nicely.'

She glared at me and I thought she was going to start again and I would have to shut the door and go downstairs and turn the television on really loud. But she didn't shout. Maybe I have a new aura of *I mean it* around me.

'No,' she said through gritted teeth.

'See, that wasn't so hard was it?' I whisked the tray

away from her. 'What about a cup of tea and a biscuit?'

She glared at me without speaking so I turned and had got to the door before she spoke.

'Yes. Please.'

'Coming right up,' I said cheerfully in my best American diner voice, and downstairs I went with a bit of a skip in my step. Even after all that running.

And that's how things have continued. I know Mother too well and I can see her plotting to put things back the way they were; she just can't figure out how to do it. She'll realise eventually that there's nothing she can do and as long as she behaves her life will continue as normal. Apart from me not putting up with her rudeness of course, but she'll get used to it. I'm making some other changes too, but not too much at once. I'll let her get used to things the way they are now and then I'll broach the subject of my wages, because I'm not giving them to her anymore. I think I'm being very reasonable; if she had to pay for a live-in carer it'd cost her an arm and a leg. I'm not expecting her to pay me – I'm just not going to pay her. But I'll leave it a couple of weeks before we have that discussion, which will no doubt cause another of her episodes.

Mrs Forsyth puts another cup of tea in front of me and I realise that I've missed most of her stories of Singapore and I'm not sure if I've given the appearance of listening. I watch her and she seems happy enough so she can't have noticed; I don't want to upset her, she's a nice lady.

'You said you've got a new client to do after me, dear?

'Yes, I have. I did a trial clean for them and they were so pleased with it they particularly asked for me.' I don't know why I'm lying, I've no reason to, I just can't seem to stop myself. It's so easy. I think I might make a hobby of it.

'That's wonderful dear. Is it once a week or twice?' Is that a hint of jealousy I can hear in her voice? I need to tone my enthusiasm down, I don't want to upset her as I am quite fond of her. It's easy money too.

'Just once. And they won't be there, they're always at work. It won't be like coming here, you know, like coming to visit a friend.' Mrs Forsyth blushes slightly and smiles and I feel a bit of a rat for playing to her like that.

'And between you and me,' I lean towards her conspiratorially, 'they're not the cleanest.'

Mrs Forsyth puts her hand to her mouth and giggles.

'Ooh, you are naughty, Alison, tell me more.'

So, I lie a bit more.

I let myself into Bella's house with the key Veronica gave me. I close the front door and stand in the hallway while I drink it all in. The pale cream walls with one wall papered in pale grey paper with large silver leaves cascading down, the deep piled cream carpet that you sink into, the faint aroma of jasmine coming from the plug-in air freshener.

I go into the kitchen and scrutinise it; reminiscent of my first visit with Doris and Rita, the worktops are littered with dirty plates, glasses and cups with not an inch of clear beechwood to be seen. A heavy copper frying pan is wedged in the sink, the remnants of bacon and eggs floating in the scummy water that's been run into it. I drain the water from the frying pan and scoop the leftovers out with a spoon and slop it onto the nearest dirty plate. I put the sink plug in and turn the taps on and run fresh hot soapy water while I scrape the leftovers from the plates into the bin. Judging by the contents of the bin they're partial to Marks and Spencer meals for two and steak, lots of very expensive pre-packaged steak. I pile the dishes next to the sink and unload the clean items from the dishwasher and reload it. Not strictly my job but I want to do it, I want this house to be perfect and I have a hard act to follow in Rita. I don't want Bella asking for someone else to clean because I've not done what Rita always does.

I wonder if I'll ever have the need to buy a Marks and Spencer meal for two? I could buy one for myself and Mother but it's hardly the same is it? Anyway, too many calories in it; maybe when I'm slim.

I clean the frying pan and then whizz around the worktops and cupboard doors with the spray and cloth until they're sparkling. I look at my watch to see that I've already used over an hour of a two-hour clean. I'm not bothered if I run over, I want to make a good impression even though I won't get paid for the extra hours. Besides, I get paid for cleaning Mrs Forsyth's and I don't do any cleaning at all there.

I slowly walk upstairs but unlike the first time I was here I take my time and use the opportunity to have a good look at everything. I go into the room that's used as a study and look at all of the stuff on the desks being careful not to touch anything. Bella's side is untidy; her pink laptop is still open at her emails and post it notes are stuck haphazardly on the notice board on the wall in front of the desk. I sit down in her seat, a squishy leather swivel chair on wheels that don't move very well on the plush carpet. I straighten my shoulders and cross my legs and pretend I'm Bella. Her laptop keyboard looks shiny with grease in places and I minimise the screen to wipe it over with a cloth but then stop myself and leave it dirty; I don't want them to think I'm prying. I don't recall seeing Rita clean it, in fact I'm sure she said something about them not wanting anything touched on the desks and just to vacuum the carpet and dust everywhere but the desks. Her partner's side of the desk, or Justin, as I discover he's called from the credit card bill lying in the 'to do' tray, is much tidier and organised. His laptop is closed and squared tidily in the middle of the desk, his chair neatly pushed underneath. A neat row of post-it-notes are soldiered along the edge of the notice board, lined up with precision.

Bella and Justin. Even sounds glamorous doesn't it?

After dusting the chairs and the windowsill and skirting boards, I stand back to make sure I've not disturbed or moved anything. Satisfied, I move onto their bedroom. I make straight for the walk-in wardrobe; Bella has so many clothes, beautiful clothes in sizes eight and ten. She has at least ten gym outfits; not cruddy leggings and baggy t-shirts like I wear but glossy black stretchy leggings shot through with lovely rainbow colours with matching zippered tops. At least five pairs of trainers, all designer names. I can't imagine Bella sweating, she'd even look beautiful working out.

I wonder what her job is; she has lots of smart suits with tiny silky blouses, lots of different coloured, high heeled court shoes. Designer jeans in every colour imaginable, several still unworn with the price tags dangling from them. I grasp hold of a pair and study the ticket and gasp at the price; several of my weeks' wages for one pair of jeans.

Dresses too, short, swingy mini-dress, knee length elegant day dresses and gorgeous, long, flowing dresses in sumptuous silks and lace.

I turn to Justin's side of the wardrobe; suits, so many suits. I can tell by the feel of the fabric that these are not run of the mill. I select a dark blue jacket with the faintest of gold pinstripes and carefully unbutton it to find the hand sewn label inside; *Gillespies of Saville Row.* Of course, handmade.

I spend far too long in the wardrobe but I can't help myself. I even look through Bella's underwear drawer – she'd probably call it lingerie. Beautiful lace and satin bras, everything matching in every colour available. I think of my own greying giant-sized cotton knickers and utility bras and feel ashamed. One day, one day.

I look at my watch to see that two hours have gone by and I've barely started. I drag myself out of the walk-in wardrobe and begin to dust, picking up discarded clothes from the floor and putting them in the huge wicker hamper in the bathroom next to the *his* and *hers* basins. I wonder if they send their laundry out? I can't imagine Bella washing and ironing.

By the time I leave the house I've been there over

three hours. I don't mind; I feel exhilarated. I feel as if I'm getting to know Bella, getting to know more about her life.

There's a lot that I don't know, of course. I don't know where she works, or where she comes from or who her friends are, or how long she's been with Justin.

But I have plenty of time to get to know her; all the time in the world.

And her passwords; I have those too. To her emails, her bank accounts, everything, really. A few clicks on my mobile phone taking photographs of her post it notes and I have it all; everything I need.

Just so I can get to know her, feel closer to her.

I'm not going to do anything *bad*, I just want to know.

I *need* to know.

I have Justin's too; his post-it-notes were so neatly arranged I only needed to take one photograph. Not that he really interests me; I probably won't bother looking at his.

But you never know.

Chapter 9

'Somefing funny going on, defo.' Doris heaps another teaspoonful of sugar into her tea and gives it a brisk stir.

'Like what?'

It's Sunday afternoon and Doris and I are sitting at our usual table in Joey's Café. Now that I've got Mother sorted out I've given myself a lot more freedom. Doris quite often texts me and suggests meeting up and I always used to say no. But not anymore.

'Dunno. But Ronnie was defo cagey about Rita, said she weren't sure wever she'd be coming back or not.'

I take a thoughtful sip of my tea, I take it black now, less calories. I don't want Rita to come back, I don't want to give up Bella.

'What's wrong with her? I asked Veronica and she was a bit non-committal.'

Doris looks puzzled, 'A bit what?'

'A bit vague.'

'Oh, yeah. Dunno. Some sort of stomach upset I fink. Not really sure, like I said, all a bit of a big fucking secret. Anyway, fing is, those two grannies in twinsets have got most of her clients and I wouldn't mind a couple of extra shifts meself.'

I keep quiet; I have no intention of offering my

shift at Bella's to Doris.

'I thought you didn't want anymore. The twinsets only took them because no one else wanted them.'

'I didn't. Then.' Doris looks downcast. 'Charlie's been laid off again.'

'Oh no, what happened?'

'Yeah, well he ain't exactly been laid off, boss sacked him. Bad timekeeping or somefing. Fucking prick.'

I don't know if she means Charlie or the boss so keep quiet.

'I dunno why I bovver with him sometimes. He's always letting me down.'

Charlie then. He lets her down all of the time but she still sticks by him; funds him until he finds another job that won't last.

'I'm really sorry, Doris. I'd let you have the Monday one but I need the money, Mother's pension doesn't stretch very far these days.'

'S'okay. Dunno why those two grannies want them, not going to do much at their age are they? They can't need the money, I mean, they're practically dead, what the fuck they gonna spend it on?'

A smartly dressed young couple look over disapprovingly at us from the table in the corner. They sit opposite each other with a pasty-faced child wedged into a pushchair alongside the table and between their seats. They're around my age but have an air of being much older. I heard them ask Joey if he had any camomile tea when they came in and when he replied it was PG Tips or nothing I thought they were going to walk out. Probably the fact that cafés are a bit thin on the ground in Frogham stopped them, never mind ones that do camomile tea. Joey thinks he's a bit of a trailblazer because he's got cappuccino on the menu. I watch out of the corner of my eye; the man pauses dramatically as he's putting his cup to his lips, and I'm sure I hear the woman tut and I half expect her to clap her hands over the baby's ears to protect him from Doris's swearing. I ignore them and hope Doris hasn't heard or noticed; to say she doesn't take criticism very well is an understatement. Doris is what Mother would call *common* or *no better than she should be*, whatever that means. I have to admit that she is loud; there's no volume button on Doris's voice at all.

'Why don't you ring Veronica tomorrow and ask her? I'm sure she'd give you one of Rita's shifts if you asked. They've got all of them apart from the one I'm doing so it's only fair that you get one. They didn't really want them anyway.'

'Yeah, fink I'll do that.' Doris looks a bit happier. 'I'll ring her first fing.'

'Good. Another cup?' Doris doesn't answer, she's too busy glaring at the couple in the corner.

'Gotta problem?' she says loudly, 'Somefing I can help you wiv?' So she did hear them; Doris's words are polite but the tone is threatening.

Not so brave now they've been challenged, the couple quickly look away and suddenly find the contents of their teas fascinating and the woman concentrates on pushing a plate with a half-eaten piece of carrot cake away from her towards the edge of the table. Razor thin with poker straight hair that reaches almost to her waist I feel an irrational dislike for her. Who leaves half a slice of cake for God's sake? Eat the lot or go without.

'I'll have a latte this time, Al, cheers,' Doris says cheerfully as I push my chair back and stand up. 'That is,' she continues loudly, staring at the couple in the corner, 'if it's alright wiv you?'

Here we go again.

When I arrive at Bella's house there's a car parked on the driveway; long, low, and sleek, it's dark, shiny grey and resembles a crouching tiger. I don't think I'd fit in it, and if I could wedge myself inside I don't think I'd be able to get back out. I park on the road, mindful of Rita's warning about taking liberties.

As I walk past the car to the front door I peer at the badge to see that it's a Porsche. I can just make out black leather seats edged in cream piping through the black tinted windows. I know that this must be Justin's car as Bella drives a powder blue open topped sports car. It's a shock that Justin is here as I wasn't expecting anyone to be home. I feel disgruntled and off balance; this will definitely impact on my day as I won't be able to take my time and immerse myself in feeling close to Bella.

God, that sounds creepy doesn't it? I'm not besotted with her or anything, I just like to imagine that I have a life like Bella's. That this house is my home instead of the miserable seventies throwback that I really live in. Now I won't be able to, he's spoilt it.

I take out the front door key and wonder whether to knock, unsure of the etiquette. I always knock at Mrs Forsyth's but she's always there, she's never been out when I've arrived and she doesn't even expect me to do anything. This is different; apart from Mrs Forsyth, I've never encountered anyone at home when I clean. I've always assumed they'd rather be out; less embarrassing to have someone clean up your dirt if you're not there. I stand outside for a moment and then decide I'll let myself in as normal; it's not my fault he's at home.

I unlock the front door and when I get into the hallway I close the front door firmly, making no attempt to do it quietly, hoping that he'll hear.

Silence.

What if he's in bed? I decide that I'll call out and if I get no reply I'll go and come back later.

'Helloo,' I call.

No answer.

'Helloo,' I shout.

Silence. After a moment there's the sound of a door opening upstairs. A pair of denim legs appear at the top of the stairs and stand there.

'The cleaner,' I say loudly, 'from Moppers. I've come to clean.'

'Of course! Sorry you threw me for a moment, I forgot you come on Mondays.'

A pair of legs descend the stairs and Justin comes into view; just as gorgeous as his photograph and a perfect match for Bella. He may not be wearing a dinner suit but the tattered jeans and faded t-shirt don't detract from his handsomeness at all.

'Hi,' I'm Justin, nice to meet you.' A flash of perfect teeth and ice blue eyes. He extends a well-muscled, tanned arm and proffers his hand.

'Hi, I'm Alison.' In my embarrassment at being in the company of a God my voice has come out all wrong and I practically shout at him. I must sound and look like a complete halfwit as I stand there gawping at him. I grasp his hand in a firm handshake and crush his fingers briefly with my now sweating hand before letting go. I can't help noticing that he brushes his palm surreptitiously down the side of his jeans as his hand drops.

He looks a bit startled but quickly recovers and hides it well. 'I'm working from home but don't mind me, you just carry on as usual. Pretend I'm not here. I'll be in my study so don't worry about cleaning it this week.'

He gives me another dazzling smile that never reaches his eyes and turns and disappears back up the stairs and I stand there like a statue watching him escape from the giantess in the hallway.

Did his mouth twitch as if he was trying not to laugh at me? I think it did. All my feelings of insecurity are back with a vengeance. I may not be supersize anymore but I still have no confidence in my appearance. I still feel like an ungainly lump. Why did I grip his hand so tightly? Why do I turn into a sweating mess the minute I feel nervous?

Depressed, I bend down and put my shoe covers on and then pick up my cleaning kit from the doormat. As I straighten up I catch sight of my reflection in the huge mirror that covers most of one wall.

I do look strange: I still wear the same t-shirts that I have always worn but they are now so big I could fit Mother in with me as well. I had to buy some new leggings (Foodco special, two pairs at two-ninety-nine each) as my old ones were so big that they wouldn't stay up, not even with a belt on. The Moppers tabard that wouldn't do up is now so big that it's become a liability and I have to take it off before I actually start any cleaning otherwise I'd spend all of my time holding it out of my way. This ensemble, topped off with a bright red, beetroot face that's slowly returning to its normal colour and wispy, flyaway hair scraped into an unflattering ponytail.

What do I look like? The village idiot, that's what.

I trundle despondently through to the kitchen to be greeted by the usual dirty dishes littered everywhere. As I unload, scrape and stack the dishwasher a feeling of resentment starts to bloom. *He's* up there tinkering around on his laptop, doing whatever it is that bankers do when they work from home (yes, I did have a peek; my curiosity got the better of me) while I'm down here clearing up his mess, which actually I'm not paid to do. He must know it's not part of my job because the contracts from Moppers are very black and white, and obvious, but he thinks that's okay, because that's all the village idiot is good for.

A loud clang makes me jump and I realise that I'm crashing the plates into the dishwater in anger. I stop and take a deep breath; calm down, I have no reason to feel peeved; no one's asked me to do this. I should report it to Veronica and she'd bring it to their attention and they'd have to pay more, and realistically, he probably doesn't even know that the cleaner is not supposed to do the washing up. Let's face it, is someone who earns nearly a hundred-thousand-pound bonus every year going to bother reading the rules on a cleaning contract? Of course not. I'm being ridiculous.

The real problem is that he's here and I don't want him here. I like to clean on my own and enjoy it. A sudden horrible thought occurs to me: what if he decides to work from home all of the time?

'Would I be getting in your way if I make a coffee?'

He's in the doorway, hovering.

'No of course not, just pretend I'm not here.' I try not to shout this time but end up saying it so quietly that I have to repeat it because he couldn't hear what I said. I should be put down. Really, I should. Not fit for purpose, that's me.

He proceeds to make himself a cup of coffee, instant, not in the fancy percolator sitting on the worktop. Probably because he wants to get away from this oddity of a cleaner as soon as possible. He doesn't offer me a coffee and he leaves the spoon on the worktop, in a splutter of coffee, for me to clear up. Like a servant, which I suppose I am. Then he disappears back upstairs to whatever it is that he's doing.

I turn on the dishwasher and fill the sink with hot, soapy water. I scrub the worktops and wipe over the cupboards until they're gleaming; and maybe I scrub them with a bit more vigour, a bit more force, as I imagine that it's Justin's perfect face that I'm scouring.

Kitchen scrubbed I go upstairs and changing my normal routine I start in their bedroom; as usual dirty clothes litter the floor and the bed is unmade, the covers pulled back and pillows all askew; left just as it was when they climbed out of it this morning.

Another job that we Moppers are not supposed to do: make beds.

I gather up the dirty clothes from the floor and take them into the bathroom to put in the laundry hamper. I close the lid and look around; toothpaste on the basin, *his* basin, scummy soap stains where he hasn't bothered to rinse it away because he's far too important to do trivial things like clean up after himself.

Well, you may be handsome, you may have perfect teeth and twinkly eyes; not that they twinkled for me, but you're a bit grubby, Justin Willoughby. You may be a highflying banker with oodles of money but I've picked your smelly underpants up off the bedroom floor, so get over yourself.

How is it that some people have everything and others, like me, and Doris, have very little? I wonder what sort of start Justin had in life, where he came from, to have all this? Was he born to it? Has he worked hard for it or was it given to him on a plate. I decide that I'll have another look later, I had a quick look when I was researching Bella but I wasn't really interested in him then.

Now I am.

I clean the bathroom, taking great pleasure in using the same cloth on the toilet and then Justin's basin, but not Bella's, obviously. I also hold his nice, expensive, top of the range electric toothbrush down the toilet and flush it and then take a moment to compose myself; it wouldn't do for him to hear the cleaner laughing hysterically alone in the bathroom.

He might think she was mad.

I whizz around the rest of the house, vacuum

every floor, except for the study, as well as mopping the kitchen. For the first time ever, I've completed the clean in two hours even with doing the extras.

Shoe covers removed and cleaning kit packed I stand on the doormat, uncertain whether to tell him I've finished. If I just leave without telling him won't that look odd? In an agony of indecision, I stand there. I don't want to speak to him, I feel uncomfortable and ungainly in his presence and I want to avoid him but common sense tells me that if it was anyone else but him I'd tell them I was finished.

Decision made I slip the shoe covers on and pad back up the stairs, determined not to make a complete idiot of myself this time. The study door is slightly ajar and I can hear a one-sided conversation; he's on the phone. Do I knock? No. I'll stick my head around the door and give a little wave and go. That'll be better; I won't have to speak then which cuts down the odds of embarrassing myself by either shouting or whispering. I move closer and catch part of his conversation, he's talking to Bella.

'….what, the cleaner? Don't know, darling, bit of a strange fruit.' He laughs and pauses, then continues talking.

I back out of the doorway silently, holding my breath, praying that the floorboards don't creak. I tiptoe down the stairs, pick up my cleaning kit and quietly let myself out of the front door, still wearing the shoe covers. Only then do I breathe out. I stand for a moment to compose myself and then pad to my car, unlock it and throw the cleaning kit onto the back seat. I rip the shoe covers off and fling them in after it, then get into the driving seat and slam the door.

Strange fruit?

Hmm. You shouldn't have said that, Justin Willoughby.

You really shouldn't.

Chapter 10

I know I said that I wasn't going to buy any new clothes until I got to my target weight but I can't carry on wearing my old clothes, I look ridiculous. The sight of myself in Bella's hallway mirror has compelled me to face facts: I need to buy some clothes that fit. I hate trying on clothes which is another reason why I've been putting it off. There's nothing worse than trying stuff on and realising that you've gone up another dress size and everything looks awful anyway. Mostly I'd buy the biggest size I could find in Foodco and just hope I'd fit into it. I know that I'm nearly at my goal and normal size clothes will fit me but I just couldn't imagine buying clothes and enjoying it.

So I trotted into Next and I thought; I'll just buy enough to keep me going until I lose that last stone. I took two pairs of the cheapest jeans I could find and four plain t-shirts from their basic range into the changing room.

I wasn't sure what size to take so I took them all in a size fourteen, which was being a bit optimistic, and a sixteen as well, which was much more realistic. The assistant at the entrance to the changing rooms said I wasn't allowed to take that many in so I gave her all of the fourteens to hold while I tried on the sixteens.

I'd only just pulled the first pair of jeans over my

legs and up to my waist when the assistant asked me through the curtain if she could help. I thought for Christ's sake give me a chance, but do you know what? I didn't even need to do them up to know that those jeans swamped me, they were *huge*. I couldn't believe it, talk about thrilled. So I got the assistant to pass me all of the size fourteens and I gave all the sixteens to her.

So there I was in that tiny little dressing room with the assistant standing on the other side of the curtain and I thought; I know that I'll struggle to get them on but as long as I can do them up I'll buy them, it'll spur me on if they're too tight, motivate me to lose that last stone a bit quicker. Maybe cut out breakfast altogether. So I stepped into them and pulled them up and there was no resistance at all. Zipped them up and did the button up and I could fit both my hands down the front they were so big. Must be a mistake, I thought, she must have given me a size sixteen back.

'Everything okay, Madam, would you like me to get you another size?'

I popped my head out between the curtains.

'Are these the sixteens you've given me?'

'No, madam, they're the fourteens but I think you probably need a twelve.'

Well, my mouth dropped open in shock and I just gawped at her. Me, a twelve, I thought I must be dreaming.

'I'll pop and get them for you.' And she silently glided off in the way that dressing room attendants do.

I sat down on that little bench in that tiny dressing room and waited and tried to figure it out. I knew I'd lost a lot, my bras are so big I've been doing them up with a safety pin and they're so baggy that I might as well have not bothered wearing them. And the only thing holding my knickers up were my two-ninety-nine leggings from Foodco which also have to be safety pinned to keep them up, but a twelve? Never.

The assistant seemed to be gone an awful long time and I was just thinking of getting dressed and going to look for her when I heard her voice through the curtain.

'Hope you don't mind,' she said, poking her head through the curtains, 'there weren't any left in the styles you chose so I selected a few different options for you.' She thrust two handfuls of hangers through the curtains so obviously the rule about taking too many in doesn't apply if you work there.

I smiled and took them off her and swished the curtain closed. The jeans felt a much nicer quality than the value ones I'd chosen, thicker material and a nicer blue too. A nice style, younger, more fashionable. I looked at the price tags to see that they were also much more expensive. Hmm, I thought, wonder if that was deliberate. I could always make do with just one pair of jeans and two t-shirts. I didn't want to spend too much because I'll need to buy all new at the end but I can't very well walk around in clothes five sizes too big, can I?

I pulled on the first pair, skinny, light blue, belly button skimming. I got them over my legs easily and over my backside but I couldn't get them done up, not even if I laid on the floor. I swallowed down the bitter disappointment. See, I knew I was fatter than a twelve and she'd gone and got my hopes up and, for a moment, I hated her.

I ripped them off bad temperedly and shook them out to put them back on the hanger. The size ten hanger. I gawped at it in disbelief; I'd actually got a pair of size ten jeans *on* and very nearly got them done up.

That was it; after that I couldn't contain myself and I came out of Next with two massive carrier bags and I'd spent over four-hundred pounds. It felt fabulous, for the first time since I was a teenager I actually enjoyed buying clothes and I just couldn't stop myself. I tried on so many jeans and tops and jumpers and they all fitted; some were size tens and some twelves and I felt so good that I couldn't choose between them. I couldn't decide which ones I wanted so I had them all. Then she started bringing shoes in to try with them, *to see how they hang*, and I put a pair of heels on and I felt so good. I wouldn't have believed that a pair of shoes could make such a difference and I vowed there and then; no more shuffling around in cheap Foodco ballet flats.

Next, she started bringing dresses to try on too, with pretty leggings and tights that she matched up with them. It was obviously a slow sales day and I think I became her project but I didn't mind at all, I probably wouldn't have had the confidence to do it on my own. She certainly knew how to put stuff together, she teamed colours and styles together that I'd never have thought of. I bought new underwear as well; underwear that actually fits and it made such a difference. My boobs looked bigger and perkier and my waist looked tiny and I've still got a stone to go. Two pretty bras with matching knickers, similar to

Bella's although nowhere near as expensive. I'll need more of course but they'll do to start with. I bought two pairs of shoes and a lovely pair of ankle boots. I felt quite sad when I'd finished trying everything and it was time to leave; I can't remember when I've had such a lovely time. The assistant whisked everything away to the till and I got dressed in my old clothes and I felt such an ugly, fat frump again. And then when I put my old size twenty-two beige anorak on over the top I thought, no, I'm never wearing that again, so I came out of the changing room and went over to the coat section and tried on a pea green three-quarter length, fitted coat in a lovely wool mixture. The assistant came over and said how lovely it looked and I know she was trying to get me to buy it but I could see myself that it did look fab, so I got her to add it to the pile on the desk at the till.

When I'd paid for it all I asked her not to put the coat in a bag as I was going to wear it and she cut the label off for me. When I finally came out of Next I crossed over the road to the car park, took that horrible beige anorak out of the Next bag and stuffed it into the bin outside Foodco.

I blew my budget massively. And although I've managed to save a bit from my wages it wasn't a huge amount so I didn't have enough money to buy all of those clothes. So, I used Mother's bank card. She won't know and when her bank statement comes I'll just rip it up and put it in the bin, but even if she finds out, so what? She can't actually do anything about it, can she? And it felt so good spending money on myself, I thought, I could get used to this and I think I might do it more often.

And as it turned out I did it a lot sooner than I expected. I reached my car and opened the boot and deposited my bulging shopping bags inside and as I closed the boot my eyes fell on the back entrance to Helicon Sports and the thought of my scruffy running gear popped into my head. I could have some nice colourful sportswear like Bella; not Foodco's basic trainers and baggy arsed joggers. I looked at my watch; quarter-to-four, plenty of time to kit myself out with some upmarket sportswear.

Armed with Mother's bank card I marched across the car park towards the shop and I thought; this is going to be fun. I'm in a good mood so I'm cooking Mother's favourite tea; pork chops and mash with cabbage and peas. Strangely enough now the pressure's off and Mother daren't complain about my cooking it's improved; she was so critical before we had our little talk but now she never moans about what I give her. I don't bother shutting the door when I use the microwave either; so what if she hears the ding, what can she do? She has been very quiet lately and I know that she's plotting; desperately trying to think of a way to get things back the way they were before; when *she* had the power.

But really, she can't; she doesn't see anyone apart from me and I've started to drop hints here and there that she might be going a bit, you know, *senile*, not right in the head. Nothing too obvious, a snippet to Veronica here, confiding to Doris that *I'm worried about Mother*, that sort of thing. I've, accidently on purpose, bumped into Dolph at Foodco a couple of times and pasted a concerned and worried expression on my face and told him how *Mother is not herself but, of course, I'd never let her go into a home.*

Dolph thought I looked different; he cocked his head to one side and pursed his lips making no effort to hide the fact he was studying me. He offered me a free haircut like he always does, and Mother too; I said I'd let him know but I won't take him up on it; don't want to get too friendly with the neighbours although they're useful for putting the story around that Mother's going doolally.

Honestly, I surprise myself sometimes with how devious I can be; as well as a liar. Maybe I take after my father. No, actually, thinking about it, I definitely take after Mother; I've learnt from the best.

I'm going straight out for a run after I've taken her dinner up to her, I don't need to wait until dark anymore and I'll have my salad when I come back. I bought four running outfits from Helicon, two new pairs of trainers and two sports bras. I spent more than I spent in Next. Tonight's outfit features glossy black leggings with yellow and black shorts over them, yellow sleeveless vest over a climate controlled long sleeved, black top and yellow and black trainers to complete the look. Although it won't make any different to my running, I feel *so* good. I think I could even turn heads for all of the *right* reasons.

My shopping bags are still sitting in the middle of my bedroom where I dumped them and I'll unpack them later. I've decided I'm going to throw every single item of my old clothes into the bin. I'd like to ceremoniously burn them all but I have to be practical. I *could* give them to the charity shop but, honestly, no one should have to wear clothes like that no matter how poor they are.

While I was putting on my new running gear and admiring the little I could see of myself in the age spotted mirror above my dressing table it struck me - how shabby and old fashioned is my bedroom? Furniture that belonged to my grandparents; we're not talking antiques here, more seventies teak effect tat. It'll all have to go; the new me can't be living in the past and sleeping in a bed that still has orange nylon sheets with a nylon duvet cover and a shagpile bedside rug for God's sake.

No. It will all have to go.

I mash the potatoes and dish them up onto the plate alongside the chops, all the while marvelling at how lovely and slim my arms look in my new glossy black top. And toned; the weights have definitely paid off. Isn't there a saying, *clothes maketh a man*, or something like that? Well, clothes definitely maketh *this* woman, that's for sure.

I put the pan in the sink and run hot water into it in preparation for the washing up when I come back from my run.

Maybe I'll get a dishwasher.

Most people have dishwashers these days, don't they?

I arrange Mother's plate on her tray with her knife and fork, salt and pepper and take it upstairs. She's sitting up in bed waiting and I pull the legs out from underneath the tray and place it over her lap.

"Your favourite, Mother, pork chops.'

She doesn't look at the chops but stares at me, mouth open, a shocked look on her face.

'Why, Mother, whatever's the matter?'

She looks me up and down and shakes her head.

109

'What have you done with yourself? You look different?'

'I've lost weight Mother, got fit.' She continues staring at me and I straighten up and move back a bit so she can get a good look. How can she not have noticed that in the last four months I've dropped at least five dress sizes? Incredible isn't it? But that's Mother for you; she never really looks at me, she only criticises and belittles.

'How? How can you have done that without me knowing?' she stutters over the words, her mouth resembling a trout gasping for air.

I smile. What is there to say?

'Where did you get those ridiculous clothes from? You're surely not going out in them.'

'I got them from Helicon Sports. Lush, aren't they? Cost me a hundred-and-fifty pound, not including the trainers, but well worth it, don't you think?'

She harrumphs, recovering quickly from the shock and getting back to her normal self. 'Where did you get that sort of money from? If you can afford to waste money on that you can pay me a bit more rent.' Really, I couldn't have planned that better if I'd tried, I've been meaning to have the conversation about money with her but not got around to it and now she's presented me with the perfect opportunity.

'I'm glad you've brought that up Mother, because we need to have a little talk about that.'

She looks at me suspiciously and I'm glad I'm going out for a run as soon as I get downstairs because she's definitely going to have one of her *episodes,* and really, I can't be doing with it.

110

'The thing is, Mother, I'm not going to be paying you rent anymore.'

She starts spluttering then, as I knew she would, but I remain calm.

'No more rent,' I go on, over her spluttering, 'As I do quite enough for you without paying you rent as well. In fact, I was even thinking that maybe you should pay *me*, for all that I do for you.'

Her face goes so red and her mouth opens and closes, that trout thing again and for a moment I feel quite alarmed and wonder if she's having another stroke.

And then that nasty little voice; you know, the one I learned from her, pipes up. *Well, would that really be so bad? Wouldn't that solve a lot of problems?*

Anyway, she's not having a stroke, it's rage that's causing the scarlet face; pure rage.

'HOW DARE YOU!' she bellows, very loudly actually, for an old woman. 'After all I've done for you.' She picks the dinner plate up in both hands and then places one hand underneath it palm-up, and I know she's going to throw it at me so I put my hand up to stop her.

'If you're thinking of throwing it, Mother, be aware that I won't be cleaning it up, or making you anything else to eat.' I speak in calm, quiet voice.

She glares at me, her mouth agog, her eyes blinking disbelief.

'Just remember, Mother,' I continue, 'that if you throw it, wherever it lands it'll stay and we're coming on for summer now, so it'll attract the bluebottles, won't it?'

She holds the plate for a few minutes in mid-air

111

and then decides that she believes me and slowly lowers it back down onto the tray. This used to be a favourite of hers when she had one of her episodes, before we had our little talk. I've cleaned many a dinner off of the wall and carpet and it's not easy to get mashed potato out of a carpet, nor tomato soup either.

'I'm going out now Mother, for a run. I'll be back in time to bring you your cocoa up.'

She doesn't speak but continues to stare at me as I come out of her room.

I think, all in all, that went rather well.

Chapter 11

You know that saying, feeling like a million dollars? Well that's how I feel. I've been and had my hair done although I didn't take up Dolph's offer of a free haircut, I went to *Hair by Maurice*, just off the precinct, not far from Moppers actually.

It's all very well having this new body and lovely new clothes to wear but it was topped off with rat bag hair which badly needed something doing to it. I can't remember the last time a proper hairdresser cut it, usually I've just hacked the ends off with Mother's dressmaking scissors and tried to tidy it up a bit. I wasn't expecting too much, just a general tidy up as you can only work with what you've got or as Mother would say, you can't make a silk purse out of a sow's ear.

A lovely girl called Kerry did it for me; when she called me through to the chair I looked at her and thought; I'm going to feel like a big ungainly lump having my hair done by her because she was so pretty and she had lovely long blonde hair – which is what you'd expect with her being a hairdresser – but I didn't feel like a lump at all, because I'm not a fatty anymore and she was so nice I think it would have been fine even if I were. I said to her, do what you like to it but I must be able to get it into a ponytail for my running and I need to be able to do it myself, and there's no point in curling it because it'll have dropped out by the time I get out of the chair. The most I was hoping for was neat and tidy.

All of these years I've thought my hair was mousey and flyaway but it turns out that it's a hairdresser's dream; not too thick so that it takes an age to cut and dry, and underneath that good old British mouse is a hint of red, which just needs treating properly to bring it out. I did ask her about having some highlights in it, a bit of colour, but she said absolutely not and why would you want to dye it when you have lovely natural highlights of your own? I really warmed to Kerry when she said that because she could have just done it anyway and charged a lot more.

As for the treating my hair properly she meant not washing it in Foodco's value shampoo, or, God forbid, *washing up liquid* (I thought Kerry was going to faint when I told her I use it if I run out of shampoo) and she says I absolutely *must* condition it every time I wash it.

She sat me in front of the mirror and did lots of fluffing and pulling up of my hair and letting it drop around my face. At one point she knelt down behind me and yanked the back down so hard my head bobbed backwards. She stood up and looked at me in a satisfied way and called for Lacey, the apprentice, who took me over to the basin and put a gown on me and sat me down. I leaned back into that backwards sink and closed my eyes and relaxed while she washed my hair in a gorgeous smelling shampoo. She rinsed it off and then put the conditioner on and gave me a mini head massage. It was divine, I nearly fell asleep. I was then whisked back over to Kerry's chair and

114

offered coffee and biscuits, which I declined. Kerry didn't cut very much off but did do lots of shaping and layering and some more fluffing, I have to say it looks and feels amazing, it falls around my face in such a flattering way, completely changes the shape of my face and I can still get it in a pony tail. Kerry has assured me that it'll be dead easy to look after as long as I use the products she advises and go back for a trim every five to six weeks.

If it's that easy I thought, why not? I bought the shampoo and conditioner from the stand they have at the desk where you pay, and a new comb and brush too, because apparently, they are so important for looking after your hair. It was nearly a hundred pounds by the time she added it all up but that was fine because I used Mother's card. I thought I deserved her to treat me after her latest episode and I also gave Kerry a nice big tip for being so nice and helpful.

Okay, so Mother didn't actually *have* an episode after the rent discussion but she's had lots of episodes in the past and they all count, don't they? All the evenings of Mother screaming at me and not letting me go downstairs to watch my programmes or eat *my* dinner. Not to mention the clearing up of those thrown dinners; all the scraping of food off the carpet and walls, and then the re-cooking of a meal that Mother graciously decides *is* acceptable. I'm not forgetting all of the nasty things she's said and all of the horrible names that she's called me. No, I think a haircut is very small compensation for all of that and she can pay for the next one too, in five weeks' time.

I came out of the hairdressers with a definite

spring in my step and the sun was shining with that lovely hint of summers-just-around-the-corner feeling. I was wearing a pair of my new skinny jeans and a white vest top with my new lovely mustard coloured sloppy Joe jumper over it, and to complete the look I had on my new soft brown leather ankle boots. As I walked down to the high street I could sense I was being looked at; although actually, I didn't so much walk as *saunter*. To be truthful, I think maybe I wanted to be looked at. I have a highly tuned awareness of people looking - I don't even have to see it, I can feel it. Years of being jumbo sized have equipped me with the knowledge that I'm being stared at without it appearing that I've noticed, a quick swivel of the eyes is all it takes. This being looked at was different though. Instead of the *Jesus look at the size of her* looks, or muffled sniggers or outright guffaws I was aware that a couple of youngish men had turned to look at me as I passed them.

They were looking at me because I looked good.

I strode along and I pushed my shoulders back just a little bit more and I think I might have even attempted a bit of a wiggle. All I needed was a lanyard around my neck, swinging away and I'd really be like Bella. Well, I would if I had a decent job; I certainly don't want a lanyard with *Alison Travis, Cleaner,* on it.

I strutted all the way along to the end of the High street where the Brotherton Estate Agents massive shop front stretches right around the corner of the building into Thackeray Street, the windows chock full of properties for sale. I stood outside and pretended to be looking at the houses for sale but really, I was looking between the edges of the house details boards to see if Bella was in there.

I could see the top of her head, the crown of her glossy blonde hair as she had her head bowed over a desk right at the rear of the shop. Even from the window I could see that her desk was the grandest; much bigger and wider and made of solid beechwood, much better than the cheap teak effect ones at the front. Partitioned from the rest of the staff by a bank of filing cabinets, making an office within an office, as befits the Sales Manager. A lot of the cheaper desks at the front were unoccupied; out on house visits probably. They must sell a lot of houses if the number of houses in the windows is anything to go by. I had toyed with the idea of going in and asking them to come out and value Duck Pond Lane but then decided against it as the Sales Manager is hardly going to do a house visit is she? And even if she did that's not really the way to make a friend is it, by getting them to value your house? Besides, I'd have to get rid of all the ghastly seventies tat and old kitchen and bathroom before I'd let Bella near it.

And Mother. I couldn't possibly let her meet Mother.

I've found out quite a lot from my research on Bella and her emails make for very interesting reading. She has thousands of emails on her account and she never, ever deletes any. And why would she? It's only her that sees them. Until now of course.

It's amazing what you can find out from someone's emails; not mine, of course, because I don't have any friends and the only emails I get, apart from bills and bank stuff for mother, are special

117

offers and junk mail. But Bella, well she's a different story altogether. I've read every one of her emails and I now have a pretty good idea of her life. Her first job at eighteen was as an admin clerk at Harpers Estate Agents which is now closed down. Nothing exciting about that except that her boss was none other than Simon Harper, also known as the Frogham Throttler, Frogham's very own serial killer.

Bella may have started as a humble admin clerk but in no time at all she was promoted to assistant sales manager. So maybe she's really clever, or lucky, but as I found some very flirty emails from Simon Harper to Bella I can't help thinking that maybe she got promoted so quickly because he liked her. Or more to the point, fancied her.

Now those emails could just be a perfectly innocent bit of office flirtation but if that was the case why did Simon Harper have Bella's personal email address and she his? The emails he sent her made it plain that he fancied the pants off her and she was very clever in her replies, never actually promising anything but never actually giving him the brush off and always a hint of *you never know what might happen in the future*. And I reasoned that if it was really so innocent any contact would have been on her office email, not her private one.

So she got promoted on a promise, really. I've no way of knowing whether she made good on that promise but that's definitely how she got on. When I realised how she got promoted so swiftly I was a bit shocked at first but then I realised that we're quite alike, Bella and I; you have to take your opportunities where you can. And that made me feel a bit closer to her, sort of sisterly. And anyway, a bit of flirtation never hurt anyone and it did the trick because before you know it she was a manager. And it doesn't mean she slept with him or anything.

Or if she did she never put it in an email and she's certainly not going to be bragging about it now is she? No one wants to admit that they've had sex with a serial killer and a pretty ugly one too. I saw pictures of him in the Frogham Herald and he's no oil painting that's for sure, and *old* too. Yuk.

Another interesting fact I unearthed is that I have more A Levels than Bella – how strange is that? She has one A level in media make-up and her GCSE results don't look too hot either. Although I did notice that on the CV that she sent for her job at Brotherton's the GCSE results have somehow improved by several grades.

This was another surprise as I expected her to have a degree of some sort although Justin, on the other hand, has more qualifications than you can shake a stick at. Some of them I'd never even heard of so I had to Google them. A proper clever clogs, as Mother would say.

Other facts that I've discovered about Bella are that she's terrible with money, always massively overdrawn and the bank's always writing to her to tell her off. All of her credit cards are completely maxed out, too. Bella earns thirty-five thousand pounds a year plus commission from her job at the Estate agents which sounds like an absolute fortune to me but it's obviously not nearly enough to buy the sort of clothes that are hanging in her wardrobe. Fortunately for her Justin earns a fortune even without his bonus so he pays all of the household bills and the mortgage, even though it's in both of their names. Her salary is basically just pocket money but it's still not enough for the designer outfits that she seems to buy every week. When trawling through her bank account I noticed that there are credits every other month or so, coming from an account in the name of G Somerton. I'm guessing that's one of her parents and they're either bailing her out on a regular basis or maybe they just like to give her money. Usually around five hundred pounds and on one occasion a thousand pounds.

Can't imagine Mother ever bailing me out. Not knowingly, anyway.

A thirty something, heavyset man in a shiny grey, cheap looking suit keeps looking up at me from his desk near the window, so I think I've loitered long enough pretending to look at houses. I know every aisle in Foodco and I can tell that the suit he's wearing is from their forty-five-pound value range. The last time he looked up he smiled at me revealing grubby looking teeth and I'm pretty sure he winked. His black hair is slicked back and with so much grease it looks like he's just been swimming. I stifle a giggle; he must think I've been looking at him. I quickly look away and meander a few steps along to the charity shop next door to gaze at the meagre offerings in their window. An assortment of bric-a-brac and framed prints are arranged over a scuffed and battered coffee table positioned in front of a faded, brown velour sofa, the sagging cushions still bearing the imprint of the many bums that sat on them.

I hear the sound of a door opening and turn to see

120

grey suit man emerging from the Estate Agents. He faces outward from the door and pulls the door shut behind him with his hand in a well-practised way and stares at me and grins. I quickly resume my charity shop pondering although I can feel his eyes on me as he's standing only a foot away. I watch out of the corner of my eye as he fumbles in his pocket for a moment and then pulls out a battered packet of cigarettes.

'Alright?' He looks over at me and smiles and I feel forced to look at him as he pops a cigarette in his mouth and lights it with a yellow plastic lighter.

'Want one?' He thrusts the battered packet towards me with nicotine stained fingers.

'Er, no thanks.'

He shoves the packet back into his pocket with a shrug, takes a deep drag and exhales noisily through his nostrils.

'Looking for a house, are you?' His head is cocked to one side, appraising me, and that's when I realise that he's come outside to talk to me.

I shake my head.

'Haven't seen you around Frogham.' He inhales another blast from his cigarette. 'And I think I know all of the pretty girls around here.'

Well, this is a first; I'm being chatted up.

'Lived here all my life.'

'Really? Can't believe I've not noticed you before.' He makes no secret of looking me up and down. So, this is what I've been missing all these years.

'Fancy coming out for a drink one night? Maybe hit the clubs?'

'I don't think my boyfriend would like it.' I lie

quickly.

'He don't have to know, do he?' He smirks, very sure of himself.

'Thanks, but no thanks. I really don't think my boyfriend would like it.'

He looks disappointed. And annoyed.

'Okay.' He takes a last puff from his cigarette and flicks the butt away and it flies into the road, red sparks jumping from it.

'Perhaps he wouldn't like you looking through windows giving other blokes the come on neither.'

Either, I want to correct him, but instead I laugh, I just can't help it. He really thought I was looking at *him*, that I fancied him.

'Don't know what's so funny, *you* were the one staring at *me*.' He buttons up his shiny grey jacket and squares his shoulders. 'You want to watch you don't send out the wrong signals.' He moves closer and looms over me and I get a blast of nicotine breath in the face. 'Could get you in trouble. There's a name for girls like you.'

I stand very still and stare at the blackheads peppering his nose.

'Sounds like a threat.'

He smirks and shrugs and steps away to go back into the Estate Agents.

'Don't flatter yourself darling, you ain't nothing special, there's plenty more where you come from. You ain't all that.'

'Do you know something,' I shout after him and he turns with his hand on the door handle and looks at me with his eyebrows raised.

'I haven't really got a boyfriend. I just don't want

to go out with you.'

His hand drops from the door handle and he steps and turns and stares at me.

'You look grubby, your breath stinks and frankly,' I laugh, 'I'm not that desperate.'

His face reddens and he moves closer to me.

'You want to watch your mouth.' He says quietly pushing his face inches from mine.

I stand very still and smile.

'No,' I say quietly, 'you want to watch yours.'

He leans closer to me with a smirk and seems about to say something but stops.

I smile again; a cold, hard smile that never reaches my eyes.

He looks at me uncertainly and backs away towards the door and opens it. He mutters something as he goes in and clangs the door shut loudly.

Sounded like *fucking bitch*.

Or maybe it was witch.

Chapter 12

When I arrive at Bella's and see that the drive is empty I breathe a huge sigh of relief. I pull the car onto the driveway and park in front of the garage and turn off the engine. I was dreading seeing Justin's car parked here as that would mean he was working from home again. He could work from home at any time, he certainly doesn't need to inform me and there'd be absolutely nothing I could do about it, but I don't like it. At least he's not here today and an uninterrupted hour is all I need. I'm relieved he's not here but a part of me wishes he was; am I really going to go through with it? My stomach flips at the thought of what I'm about to do.

I get out of the car and grab my kit and lock the car door while looking around the street. My heart is beating faster than normal and I tell myself to calm down; As far as anyone else is concerned I've every right to be here, it's my normal cleaning day. It's only me who knows what I'm going to do and only me who can mess it up. I take a deep, calming breath and walk up to the front door and let myself into the house. I close the door and once I've put my shoe covers on I place my cleaning kit right up against the door. It won't prevent anyone from getting in but it will act as an alarm, give me a few minutes' warning.

I check the downstairs rooms to make sure there's

no one in even though I know they're both at work; no one here. I run up the stairs and check all the bedrooms and bathrooms, going right into the rooms to make sure no one is hiding behind the doors.

I need to get a grip or abandon this plan altogether.

No. It'll be fine. I'm going to do it.

Satisfied that I'm completely alone I go into the study and sit down at the desk in front of Justin's laptop. As I pull on a pair of Moppers white cotton gloves, *for polishing delicate silverware*, I feel thankful for my continued good luck – sometimes when I check the study Justin's laptop is missing because he's taken it to work. I need him to take it to work for my plan to work, but not today.

I turn the laptop on and flex my fingers to get them used to the gloves. The screen comes to life and I tap in Justin's password.

It doesn't take me very long to do what I have to do; I researched it all at home and have mentally rehearsed over and over in my head exactly what I need to do. I take out my phone and scroll down the photographs until I reach the pictures of Justin's credit card; a spur of the moment action a couple of weeks ago when I found his wallet which he'd left on the coffee table. I couldn't tell you why I took the photographs, or the ones of his driving license and all of his other cards. Just in case, I suppose. Or was the idea germinating in the back of my mind even then? I don't know.

I carefully enter his card details and wait while it whirs away processing the details; I'm using his credit card rather than his debit card because I'm hoping that he won't check his credit card transactions until he gets his bill. If he's one of those that checks daily or before his laptop stops working then my plan won't work, but there's nothing I can do about that so it's pointless worrying about it. There's no way he can trace the credit card usage to me so the *worst* that can happen is that my plan won't work. I don't think he will check every day though, he earns so much he doesn't need to.

The screen seems to be taking a long time; the butterflies are starting to flutter again in my stomach when the whirring symbol finally stops and another screen pops up, *your card provider requires your verified online banking password*. I tap it in and cross my fingers that he hasn't changed it. Most people rarely change their password unless forced to, according to an article I read recently in *The Mail*, and even then, they often only change it by one digit. The screen whirs again briefly and then a new message informs me that *your purchase is complete and your receipt has been emailed as requested*. Success! The receipt will go to the fake email account that I set up in Justin's name.

Job done, I clear the search history for today and log out and close the laptop down. I lean back in the chair and stretch my arms above my head and link my fingers together to pull the tension out of my shoulders. It took even less time than I planned and I sit for a moment and stare at the blank screen as I allow myself to imagine the events unfurling if everything goes according to plan.

Okay, enough daydreaming. Now for the next stage; I rummage in my tabard pocket and realise that I didn't bring the screwdriver upstairs with me. I jump up from the chair and run down the stairs into the hallway. I quickly look out of the side window by the door to check that no one has come home while I've been upstairs; only my car sits on the drive. Good. I bend down and am opening my cleaning kit when a sudden burst of anxiety hits and my heart starts to hammer as I root around the bag. What if he comes back now and catches me? The clutter in my cleaning kit merges and black spots dance before my eyes. I feel light headed and for a horrible moment I think I'm going to faint. I slowly stand up and lean my head against the cold glass of the door and take a deep breath.

Why would Justin or Bella come home? And if they did what would they find? They'd find a cleaner, cleaning their house just like she always does. I'm being stupid, panicking for nothing. Don't ruin it now when you're so close, I tell myself, calm down and get a grip, you're nearly there. I take a deep, calming breath.

After a few minutes my breathing is under control and I check the window again; all clear. I bend down to the cleaning kit and force myself to slowly look through the contents until I spot the screwdriver nestling underneath a pack of dusters. I pull it out and go back upstairs and into the study. I trace the charger from the side of the laptop down to the electric socket underneath the desk. I unplug the charger from the socket and pull it out and crawl backwards from underneath the desk being careful not to bang my head. I get up from the floor and sit down in the chair and place the plug on the desk. I turn it over in my hand and study it for a moment and then push the end of the screwdriver into the back of the plug and flick the fuse out of it. I place the fuse on the desk; I need to stop it from working but I don't want it to be too obvious. I pull a duster out of my pocket, place it on the desk and put the fuse in the middle and then wrap the duster over it. Using the plastic handle of the screwdriver I gently bash the fuse through the duster. Even though I'm doing it gently the noise is horrifically loud so I pick it up and place it on the carpeted floor and bash it again.

Much better, no noise at all. I hit it a few more times and then take the fuse out of the duster and put it back in the plug. I scramble back under the desk and push the plug back into the wall socket and turn it on; the red light on the charger flickers red and then goes out. I turn it off and pull the plug out of the socket and then push it back in again and turn it on; nothing, the light doesn't come on this time. Satisfied that it's not working I push the flex back into the position it was, being careful not to leave it dangling, and then arrange everything back on the desk just as it was when I arrived.

Once the laptop has run out of charge it won't charge up again and I'm taking an educated guess that Justin isn't the sort to dismantle a plug to see what's gone wrong. For my plan to work he needs to take his laptop into work and get IT to fix it. I've made it pretty easy for them to find out why it's not working and any self-respecting IT geek will be onto Justin in no time at all. I smile to myself as I think of the password to the account I've created for him: strangefruit.

That'll learn him, as Doris would say.

I get up and push the chair back under the desk and have a last look around the room to make sure I haven't left anything behind. I go back downstairs and pull the cotton gloves off and bury them and the screwdriver at the bottom of my cleaning kit, no tempting fate by meaning to do it later and then forgetting and leaving them here. I look at my watch; it's taken me just over an hour, pretty good going.

I go into the kitchen and begin unloading the dishwasher and putting away the cutlery and dishes. The kitchen is the usual bombsite of dirty dishes piled haphazardly around the room; for well off people they live like pigs.

For someone who has everything that a girl could possibly want – good looks, a career, a lovely home and a catch of a boyfriend (well, for now, anyway), I can't help thinking that Bella doesn't seem to appreciate it. She has wardrobes full of beautiful clothes, clothes that cost a fortune, and she just drops them on the floor or scuffs them into a corner as if they're nothing. If they were mine I'd look after them, take care of them.

Bella doesn't deserve everything she's got.

I stop, mid scrape, plate and knife hovering over the bin and realise that I've criticised Bella; that I'm feeling disappointed in her.

I put the plate and knife down on the worktop with a sorry feeling that Bella's let me down. Everything I've done, I've done for her. The weight loss, the running, the job, the hair and clothes. I've done it all for her. If it wasn't for Bella I'd still be a big fat Nelly whose daily highlight is binge eating in front of the television. I've put Bella on a pedestal but she's falling off it. Or teetering a bit.

But I haven't done it for her, have I? I've done it *because* of her and there's a difference. *I* put her on a pedestal, no one else, and I know she's not perfect because I've seen her emails, her chaotic finances and the way she's got promotion.

And no one's perfect, are they? I'm certainly not, a little voice pipes up, because what about what you're doing to Justin? I'm not doing that for Bella, I'm doing that for me and no one else. Revenge, pure and simple that's what that is, revenge for insulting me, for laughing at me. But everything else was *because* of Bella not *for* her, my whole focus has been on being like her and now I'm starting to realise that she's not perfect, because nobody's perfect. If I really thought Bella was perfect and I wanted to be like her I wouldn't have done what I've done, would I?

While I clean the kitchen, I reflect on the changes since I first saw Bella; she's helped me, there's no doubt about that, but maybe I could take her off the pedestal and bring her down to my level, make us more equal.

But I still feel a bit adrift; what do I want? I wanted to be just like Bella, *be* Bella. I look much better than I used to; I'm slim and pretty in my own way, although not in Bella's league. But I don't have her life, her house, her job, her boyfriend.

I sigh, what do I want?

I've cleaned the whole kitchen without being aware of what I'm doing so I stomp upstairs and go into their bedroom; bed unmade, clothes on the floor, the usual squalor. I walk through the bedroom to the dressing room and survey the mess in there; wardrobe doors open, clothes half hanging off the hangers, discarded clothes on the floor that were obviously dragged out to wear but weren't quite right so were flung aside and are now crumpled and un-wearable.

I walk over to the wardrobe and pull a couple of dresses back onto the hangers and force them back in between all of the clothes packed tightly together.

Too many. Far, far too many clothes for one person.

The wardrobes run the length of the room and I walk to the far end and open the doors of the furthest wardrobe; this must be the wardrobe for the clothes that Bella seldom wears. Tightly packed hangers of dresses and jeans, blouses and jackets. I pull out a couple of dresses; one is knee length and made of green silky material, the other a light knitted dress in a mink colour.

I swing around to full length mirror behind me and hold the green dress up in front of me.

It's gorgeous.

Absolutely gorgeous. Why would she not wear this? Because she has too many, that's why. One person can't possibly wear these many clothes, especially when they keep buying more.

I rip off my t-shirt and leggings. I step into the dress and pull it up and push my arms into the sleeves. I reach behind me and after several minutes of wriggling around I manage to zip it up.

It's snug. But it's a size ten.

I study my reflection in the mirror and I hardly recognise myself; the green dress clings to every inch of me, but in a good way. I marvel at the toned woman looking back at me; she is unrecognisable from the sad, fat creature of five months ago. I move closer to the mirror, admiring myself, turning this way and that.

It's the colour; the green makes my eyes come alive and they seem huge and mesmerising. I can't pull my gaze away from my reflection. I feel good in my new clothes from Next but this, this is a whole new level.

A feeling of hopelessness swamps me. You will never have this, that doubting voice pipes up, you'll never be able to afford clothes like this or a life like this.

You'll never really be like Bella.

I turn from the mirror and reach behind me and pull down the zip and step out of the dress. I put my leggings on and pull my t-shirt over my head.

Know your place, that nasty little voice pipes up again. *Don't fool yourself.*

I zip the dress up and hang it carefully back on the hanger and attempt to push it back into the wardrobe. I get it in but it crumples and catches on the dress next to it. It deserves more than this, it deserves space to hang.

Would Bella even notice if it wasn't here?

Of course she wouldn't. She has so much she won't remember one dress. Besides, we could almost be sisters and one day we'll be friends, won't we? Decision made, I pull the hanger back out and slip the dress off it and carefully roll it up into a neat, silky package. I run down the stairs and open my cleaning kit and carefully wrap it in a bin bag and then nestle it on top of the dusters.

I am a thief.

Yes, I know I use Mother's bank card but that hardly counts; that's not theft it's compensation for the years of unpaid drudgery.

I should feel bad, I know; for what I did on Justin's laptop and for stealing from Bella.

But I don't.

I feel great.

Chapter 13

I knew everything was going too well. I also knew that when one thing went wrong that wouldn't be the end of it; bad things always come in threes.

The day started well enough, Friday is a good day, normally. Into the office to hand in my timesheet and then to the café with Doris. I'd made sandwiches for Mother's lunch so I didn't have to hurry back. I told her I'd be back in time to make dinner. Probably. It's not like she's going to starve is it?

As I came out of the house and unlocked my car a movement caught my eye and I turned to the side and sitting on the brick wall running around our garden was a magpie; calm as anything. It didn't even move when it saw me, just stared back at me with those malevolent eyes. A little part of me knew then; call it an old wives' tale if you like but there must be something in it or how do these sayings start? One for sorrow.

I shook it off and told myself to stop being so stupid but it did put a dampener on the day for me, it was there at the back of my mind. Fridays are my favourite day of the week and I cursed myself for turning around and seeing it; maybe everything would have been alright if I hadn't seen it. I prayed for a black cat to cross my path on the way to Moppers to counteract it, but of course it didn't.

The usual crowd are squeezed into Moppers when I arrive and I have a job to get through the door; most people drop their timesheets and run so I wonder why everyone is hanging around. I'd just handed over my timesheet to a miserable Moira when Doris pushed her way through the throng.

'Fuck me, what's everyone doing here?' Doris thrust her timesheet in front of Moira's nose.

Moira sniffed disapprovingly and took the paper from her.

'I don't know.' I looked down at Moira. 'Do you?'

Moira doesn't answer immediately, just to make sure we know she's superior, then says, 'Veronica wants to talk to you all.'

The malevolent magpie pops straight into my head and I know bad news is coming; Are we all getting the sack? Is Moppers closing down?

The manager's office door opens and Veronica stands silently like a Roman emperor in the doorway while she waits for the babble of chatter to stop.

'Ladies,' she announces when everyone's quiet, 'a quick announcement, if you please.'

'Get on wiv it for fucks sake.' Doris hisses under her breath.

Veronica glares in our direction; ears like a bat.

'I'm pleased to tell you that Rita, one of our longest serving employees, is coming back next week.'

My heart plummets; much worse than I feared, I hadn't even *thought* about Rita coming back. A few people murmur *good* and *nice to hear* but not, I notice, the cleaners who have taken over her shifts.

'Now I know that some of you have been doing Rita's shifts in her absence but I don't want you to worry, I have several new clients to replace those shifts if you want the hours.'

A few worried faces look happier at this news, even the pearl and twinset twosome who had to be persuaded to take Rita's shifts in the first place but wouldn't let Doris have any.

'Would those involved stay behind and everyone else can go.'

Doris taps my arm. 'I'll wait outside.'

'Why don't you stay? You could get one of the new clients.'

'Can't be arsed, Charlie's got another job now anyway.'

She joins the bottleneck of people and pushes her way out of the office.

'Ladies,' Veronica is speaking again. 'Rita will be taking all of her shifts back straight away so if you want hours to replace them please let me know now.'

She looks at us expectantly.

'Can't Rita have the new clients and we keep the old ones,' I say as I mentally cross my fingers.

Veronica looks shocked.

'I'm afraid not, they're *Rita's* clients.'

Yeah, and she's been off for two months, I want to say, but don't.

'So.' Veronica poises her pen over her clipboard. 'As from next week you're no longer cleaning at the Willoughbys' but I can offer you another shift at the same time on the other side of town. Is that okay?'

'No,' I say ungratefully. 'Leave it for now, I'll have a think about it.'

'Oh.' Veronica makes a show of crossing my name out on her clipboard. 'I can't promise you another shift if you don't take it now.'

I pick my bag up from Moira's desk and shrug. 'Whatever.'

I pull up in front of our house, kill the engine and sit for a moment. I met Doris for our usual catch up at Joey's Café but my heart wasn't in it. All I could think about was not going back to Bella's again. Was it my own fault? The last time I cleaned there had been strange; apart from the laptop shenanigans and stealing the dress. I'd started to feel a bit disgruntled with Bella, I was in a bad mood with her, thinking that she didn't deserve all that she had because she didn't take care of the house or her lovely possessions. Had those negative thoughts somehow whirled around and made Rita come back to work?

Ridiculous! Screams the rational part of me, complete nonsense! But I can't shift the feeling that somehow I made it happen. Yes, I do feel differently about Bella but that's only to be expected because I've changed; our relationship has moved on from hero worship to a more equal footing.

I still have online access to Bella's emails and accounts but I can no longer get into her house; not legally, anyway.

Although I do have a key. I had one cut, just in case.

It won't be the same, though, I won't be able to go there legitimately. I won't have a reason to be there and there'll always be the fear of getting caught.

Doris kept asking me if I was alright when we were at the café, that's when she wasn't prattling on about Charlie. Talk about a loser; what does she see in him?

I try to make hints that he's a waste of time and she should get rid but she's so loyal it's unbelievable. Love is blind in her case, that's for sure.

I obviously couldn't tell Doris what was really bothering me so I made up a story about Mother, about how she's got a lot worse and I might have to think about putting her in a home as she's acting strangely and keeps forgetting who I am. I got a bit carried away and Doris was so sympathetic; I even squeezed a few tears out.

I should be on the stage, really.

It was only a temporary diversion though; I feel deflated and adrift, and also annoyed with myself for making it happen by thinking bad thoughts about Bella.

I get out of the car and walk despondently up the path to the front door. I notice Dolph out of the corner of my eye but deliberately don't turn my head so I can pretend I haven't seen him. I hope he hasn't seen me, I don't want to talk to anyone else today. I'm just about to put my key in the lock when I hear him call out.

'Alison!'

I turn my head to see Dolph striding up the path towards me, all long rangy steps and flamboyant arms flying everywhere. He has a new hairstyle; the sides shaved close to his scalp with the top sculpted into perfect curls.

'Alison, darling, how are you?' he catches hold of my hand and spins me around so he can look at me. 'You look fabulous, darling! Fab-u-lous!'

I smile half-heartedly. 'Thank you.'

'You're positively tiny! You must tell me your

secret so I can get rid of all this blubber.' He pats his non-existent stomach and I consider telling him the truth – near starvation and running around Frogham for hours and hours until I'm fit to drop.

'But sweetheart,' he steps closer and peers into my face. 'What's the matter? Have you been crying?'

'No, I'm fine, honestly.' Have I been crying? Maybe I have.

He leans towards me and puts an arm around my shoulders, 'Is it, you know.' He looks around to make sure no one is listening. 'Your mother?' He mouths the words without sound and in spite of my misery I stifle a giggle which I quickly turn into a sob.

'Oh dear.' Dolph's eyebrows furrow in sympathy. 'You poor thing, why don't you come into mine and have a cup of tea? Brian might even have baked one of his lemon meringues.'

'Thank you, but I can't,' I say in my best *trying to be brave voice.* 'I need to get in and see to Mother.'

'Hmm, I can help out you know, take the strain off you if you need some time on your own. I could sit with her for a few hours.'

Warning bells clang, I need to be very careful. I can't have people coming in to the house and speaking to Mother.

'Thank you, Dolph, that's really sweet of you but I couldn't ask you to do that.'

'You're not asking, darling, I'm offering.'

Shit. This can't happen. That sodding magpie.

I bite my lip and frown in what I hope look like an agony of indecision look.

'The thing is, Dolph,' I say hesitantly. 'If Mother sees anyone but me she's likely to have one of her episodes. I've tried getting carers in and it was an absolute disaster.' I risk a quick look at his face; he looks a bit worried. 'I feel really disloyal saying this because I know she can't help it, bless her, and I hope you won't repeat this, for Mother's sake, but the last carer we tried had to stay off sick for a week after Mother had finished with her.'

A look of horror flashes over Dolph's face which he quickly tries to hide but I've seen it.

'Oh, that's so awful, lovey. It must be so difficult for you.'

'It's not been easy, I'll admit,' I say. 'Although luckily she agreed not to press charges otherwise I don't know what would have happened.' I let my bottom lip quiver so Dolph knows how awful it was.

Dolph stares at me in shock and I can see his mind whirring as he tries to imagine what Mother might have done. I'm almost disappointed when he doesn't ask as this is the most fun I've had all day.

'Well you know best, sweets,' he says hurriedly. 'You just let me know if there's anything I can do.' He's already backing away down the path.

'Thank you, Dolph, that means a lot.'

'Anytime, lovey, anytime.' He's already reached the garden wall and I breathe a sigh of relief; there'll be no more offers of help from him.

I watch him hurry down to his house and half expect him to break into a run. That's what people are like; all that talk about helping but not really meaning it. I've been looking after Mother for the last ten years and never had a genuine offer of help and the few friends I did have soon vanished.

Dolph disappears through his front door and no

doubt is already regaling Brian with the goings on at number six. I unlock the front door, go inside and close it firmly then pick the post up from the mat and go into the lounge and flump onto the sofa. Right now, I could eat and eat and eat. Only the fact that there's no junk food in the house stops me. I should go for a run; a good, long run. For hours and hours.

The house is quiet; usually I can hear the murmur of Mother's television which she has on from early in the morning until late at night when I turn it off after she's fallen asleep. But the house is silent and I wonder if she's okay. She could have passed away in her sleep while I was out, I mean, she's not getting any younger, is she?

I get up to go and check on her when I realise I still have the post in my hand. I look at the three letters without interest; Mother's bank statement, an offer of a credit card addressed to Mother and strangely, a letter addressed to me.

I *never* get post.

I turn the letter over in my hand and scrutinise it; my full name and address and it has a stamp on it so I know it's not junk mail. The envelope is good quality, thick white textured paper. I hold the letter in my hand and study my name and address as if the answer to what's inside will suddenly present itself to me. I quickly turn the envelope over and peel the flap back and carefully pull out the contents; one thick white sheet of textured paper. I unfold it and open it out; *Thompson's Solicitors and Commissioners of Oaths* is printed in curly black lettering across the top of the page with an address in Frogham underneath.

141

Dear Miss Travis
We are very sorry to inform you that your father,
George Henry Patterson, has recently passed away.
Please accept our sincere condolences for your loss.
We have been informed that you are his next of kin
and as such there are various matters to discuss with
you. Can you therefore please telephone this office at
your earliest convenience to arrange an appointment.
Yours sincerely
Gerald Thompson
Partner

I stare at the letter open mouthed, trying to take in what the words mean. I don't know which is more shocking – the fact that my father is dead or that he's put me as his next of kin. I've never met him, he's never contacted me or written to me in my life yet he knows where I live – that's probably because Mother has stayed here all of her life. I don't know what to make of it. He's never attempted to contact me when he was alive. Why? It just doesn't make any kind of sense.

I'll never meet him now. I'll never have the chance to find out the truth about why he 'cleared off' as Mother puts it. Bitter regret rises in my throat; too late, I've left it too late. I thought I had all the time in the world, thought that one day I would meet him. Although I made no attempt to find *him*. I was waiting for him to contact me; I was sure that he would, one day. Always at the back of my mind was the idea that one day we would meet when the time was right and his reasons for abandoning me would be explained, and of course there would be a good reason, and we'd all live happily ever after.

But not now.

If he knew where I was why didn't he contact me? Did he care anything at all about me? I veered between believing that he didn't care because he ran away and never made contact or that somehow he'd been prevented from contacting me, I could never quite decide. But if he didn't care why would he put me as his next of kin?

Why?

I need answers and I'm not going to get them from him now, am I?

I pull my mobile out of my handbag and tap in the number of the solicitors on the letter and let my fingers hover over the call button. I think for a moment and then delete the number.

Mother.

First, I need to speak to Mother, see what lies she has to tell me, find out if she's known where my father was for all of these years. How humiliating will it be to make an appointment at the solicitors and have them know that I've never met my father and know nothing about him? Or do they know already?

I stand up and walk out into the hall and stand at the bottom of the stairs for a moment. Calm down, I must compose myself before I go up there. Knowing my luck Mother *has* died in her sleep and I'll never know. *I could live with that*, that nasty little voice pipes up, *I could live with not knowing if she was dead.*

I push the nasty voice away and take a deep breath in through my nose and exhale slowly through my mouth several times, focusing my gaze on the treads of the stairs.

Which is when I see it; a peach thread caught on the carpet fibres of the second step. I bend down and catch hold of the thread and pull it out. I straighten up and hold it in my fingers and scrutinise it; only two inches long it's the exact colour of Mother's dressing gown.

I close my eyes for a moment.

The magpie.

Bad things come in threes.

Rita's back and taken over Bella's cleaning.

My father is dead.

Mother's been downstairs.

Chapter 14

Mother knew that I'd be out until late this afternoon; I'd made her sandwiches for lunch and told her that I'd be back in time to make her dinner. She knew that she had most of the day on her own.

But how? How did she manage to get downstairs? She's always been able to get to the bathroom on her own but never bothered unless she's desperate; too afraid of falling and hurting herself and ending up in hospital. Also, she likes me to be at her beck and call. She can't be as disabled as she pretends to be.

It must have taken her forever to get downstairs and even longer to get back up, she must have dragged herself on her elbows. She's determined, I'll give her that. Motivated. Maybe that's where I get it from. I have a sudden panicked thought; the phone – what if she's called someone? I rush back into the lounge and look at the phone holder on top of the mantelpiece; empty.

Panicked, I scan the room and see the handset lying on the coffee table on top of a magazine. Was that where I left it? I can't remember. I pick the phone up press the last number redial button and hold it to my ear.

Nothing. The phone is dead.

Think. When was the last time I used the phone?

It very rarely rings, and on the rare occasion I

make a call I use my mobile. Wednesday, that's it, on Wednesday I answered a call from someone selling water softeners. I remember I told them I wasn't interested, hung up and then tossed the phone onto the sofa next to me, not the coffee table.

Which proves she's been down here. Luckily for me the battery has died because it wasn't in the charger, bad luck for Mother. I pick the handset up and put it back on the stand.

Luck has been on my side this time but I need to make sure this never happens again. I knew she was plotting but I've become over confident, got too sure of myself and thought that it was impossible for Mother to get the better of me. I've underestimated her and only complete luck has prevented the end of my new life.

I go out into the hall and stand silently and listen; no sound of Mother's television from upstairs. This alone should have alarmed me enough to rush up there, instead I was distracted by that solicitor's letter. I knew something wasn't right when I came in, her television is always on, all day and every day. Even if she'd taken ill it would still be blaring because the first thing she does on waking is point the remote and turn it on; it stays on until I turn it off when she goes to sleep at night. She must have turned it off so she could hear if I was here.

I slip my shoes off and walk quietly up the stairs and pad silently along to her bedroom. The door is nearly closed, only an inch gap; more evidence that she's been out of her room as I always leave it half open. I stand at the door and listen; I can hear the sound of her breathing. She doesn't snore but

146

breathes heavily when she's asleep, blowing the air noisily out of her mouth.

I think she's pretending; the breathing is too rhythmic, too perfect. I slowly open the door and step into the room. The curtains are half open as normal, she wouldn't be able to reach over the dressing table to move them and the mirror covers a good portion of the window anyway. The mirror blocks a lot of the light out but Mother wouldn't hear of me moving it, she likes semi-darkness, says it's more restful.

In the half-light I can see her face is turned to the wall and she has the eiderdown pulled up tight around her neck, just the top of her grey hair peeping out. This confirms that she's not asleep; she normally sleeps on her back, mouth open, arms by her side. Like a corpse.

I snap the light switch and the harsh glare of the ceiling light illuminates the room.

'I know you're not asleep Mother so you can stop pretending.'

Her breathing doesn't alter.

'I know you've been downstairs.'

The pretend breathing halts for a moment and then with a grunt of effort Mother turns over onto her back, opens her eyes and stares at me.

I walk over to the bed and stand over her. 'Don't bother denying it.'

She hauls herself up onto her elbows and I watch her with interest, making no move to help her.

'Aren't you going to help me?' I'm surprised at the plaintive tone in her voice; I'd expected nastiness, shouting.

'You've managed to get downstairs so I'm sure you

147

can sit up on your own.'

She doesn't move and we stare at each other.

I finally give in and walk over to the bed and grab hold of her underneath the arms and sit her up. I pull her forward and plump the pillows behind her and then settle her back onto them. She takes a long, silent look at me.

'How did you know?'

I laugh. 'You left too much evidence Mother, made it too obvious.'

'I'm not naturally devious like you.' Ah, the nastiness is still there.

'Must have taken you a long time,' I say. 'I'm surprised you managed to get down the stairs and even more impressed that you got back up them.'

'I don't know how I did it either. It certainly took it out of me.' She does look exhausted. And old.

'Why? What did you intend doing? Ringing the police? Tell them I'm keeping you prisoner?'

She shrugs. 'I don't know.'

'Yes, you do. If you want me to leave, just say the word and I'll go and live somewhere else. You can pay for carers or go into a home, you only have to say the word.'

A complete lie but I say it with confidence. There's no way I'm leaving but she doesn't know that.

'Maybe that would be for the best,' I continue with a smile when she doesn't answer. 'I could have a life then and you can get a stair lift and go downstairs whenever you want. I could give them a ring if you like, get them to come out and give you a quote. You decide. I'm not bothered, I've got a job now, I can easily find somewhere else to live.'

Mother looks uncertain, not sure if I'm bluffing.

'There's no need for you to move out,' she says. 'If we had a stair lift I could come downstairs and I wouldn't feel so isolated. We could watch TV together – I could help, you know, with a bit of dusting and that. Be like it was before I had the stroke."

Ah yes, that idyllic life before she was ill. I remember it well; I couldn't so much as *move* without her permission. She doesn't fool me with her pathetic act; she's being nice to try and get what she wants but I don't trust her one bit. The threat of my leaving is working for the moment but I know Mother; once she's got her own way it won't stop there, she won't be happy until things are back the way they were before. The sweet little old lady act doesn't take me in; give her access to a phone and my access to her account will be blocked and she'll have the doctor and social services around here in a flash.

'Anyway,' I say. 'Enough of that, we have more important things to talk about.'

She looks confused, unsure where this is going.

'Like my father, for instance.'

Mother's lips clamp even tighter and her eyes narrow.

'I have nothing to say about *him*.'

'No? Well, apparently, he's died and I'm his next of kin. Or so the solicitor's letter says.'

She doesn't bat an eyelid, no acknowledgement at all of the death of my father and her one-time lover. She glares at me in defiance.

'Nothing to say at all? Because what I'm wondering, Mother, is why he'd put me as his next of

149

kin when he's never even met me or made any attempt to contact me.'

She still says nothing.

'So you've nothing to say?'

'No.'

'Okay.' I walk over to her dressing table and attempt to pull out the top drawer, but it's locked as usual.

'Where's the key Mother?'

'There's nothing in there that concerns you.' She tightens her crossed arms across her chest.

'Okay. Last chance, Mother, give me the key or I'm going to get a crowbar and break it open.'

She sits silently and can't hide the hint of a smile on her face.

She doesn't believe me; even now she still thinks she can control me. I could look for the key, there are only so many places that she could hide it but I won't give her the satisfaction of watching me grubbing through her things to find it. Attacking the dressing table with a crowbar suddenly seems very appealing.

Without another word I leave the room and run down the stairs. I don't even know if we have a crowbar, or actually, what a crowbar even looks like but there must be something that I can break the drawer open with.

I go into the kitchen, yank open the cupboard door and start pulling the clutter out from under the sink. Bleach, washing powder, a myriad of cleaning sprays and old dusters. The only tools are a plunger and a bottle brush and they aren't going to do it are they? Would a kitchen knife do it? I dismiss the idea immediately; the dressing table is old and built when furniture was made to last a lifetime. The knife would probably break first.

I know where there are some tools but I don't want to go there. Grandfather's toolbox is in the cellar, along with all of the other old rubbish that we've never got rid of. I hate going down into the cellar and I haven't been down there for years, it's cold, damp and full of spiders. Small and dark, it doesn't even have a proper floor, just compacted earth.

I'll have to go down there though or she's won. I go out into the hall and put my shoes back on in readiness and go into the dining room. The door is hidden behind the heavy Welsh dresser that I dragged in front of it shortly after Mother had her stroke. So that I wouldn't have to see it or think about it ever again.

The key is in a jug on the top shelf of the dresser; a large, yellow hued pottery jug that I have vague memories of being filled with gravy for our Sunday roasts. I take the jug down from the shelf and put my hand in and pull the key out and put it in my jeans pocket. I then remove all of the plates and crockery from the dresser and place them on the dining table.

It would have been so much easier if Mother had given me the key but I won't give her the satisfaction of asking her for it again.

Dresser emptied I stand at one end and attempt to push it; it doesn't budge an inch. When I put it here I had a lot more weight to put behind it. I decide the best thing to do is try and drag it out from the doorway to give myself just enough room to get in there.

Somehow, I manage to pull it out from the wall by about a foot; this should be enough as the cellar door opens inwards.

I take the key out of my pocket and squeeze behind the dresser, the door is only a foot along from the edge of the dresser and I shuffle behind it until I'm in front of the door. I push the key in and turn it and the door flies inward and a blast of cold dank air hits me. I carefully put the key back in my pocket and grope with my hand around the doorway onto the cellar wall until I feel the familiar shape of the old Bakelite switch. I press it down, praying that the bulb still works; if it doesn't then I'm not going down there. I'll have to search Mother's room for the key, instead.

A weak light from the bare bulb throws the middle of the cellar into view, the corners of the room in darkness. I should have bought a torch with me. I know if I go back to get one I won't have the nerve to come in here again. I take a deep breath and step gingerly onto to the stone cellar steps. Ten steps down. How many times did I count those steps when I was a child? I look above me to make sure there aren't any cobwebs, or God forbid, spiders. Treading carefully down the steps, making sure not to slip, I grip the wooden handrail, shiny and slippery with age. When I reach the bottom, I stop and look around me and wonder why I'm doing this to myself.

A memory jolts me and I am five-years-old again; Mother has shut me in here for misbehaving. I am terrified of the dark, of spiders, of being alone. I'd stand here on the cellar steps, shivering and crying, too afraid to sit down in case the spiders got me.

Terrified that she'd forget about me and leave me here forever. Mother said I was a drama queen, said she'd been locked down here many times when she was a child and it never did her any harm, did it?

She said I was *weak*; that the cellar wasn't haunted so what was I afraid of? Of course, as soon as she said that I was afraid there were ghosts too. I very rarely misbehaved after the first time she locked me in, the threat of the cellar enough to deter me. I must have been like a robot child, one look from Mother and I did exactly what I was told.

Mother liked it when I was frightened of her – and that *does* make me sound like a drama queen, but it's true. If I wet the bed or fell over and grazed my new shoes, that too ensured a spell in the cellar *to teach me a lesson*.

Is it any wonder I've spent most of my life doing exactly what she says? I shudder, the dampness seems to permeate my very skin and I wonder if the ghosts of my grandparents are watching me.

Enough.

Too many years of being afraid; time to grow up now. I scan the room for signs of a tool box, the far wall looks likely; an ancient sideboard is piled high with boxes, old lampshades and assorted debris. As I move closer to the sideboard out of the corner of my eye I see something scuttle across the floor and then freeze in the middle of the room. I slowly turn my head to see an enormous black spider crouched a foot away from me. It senses me looking at it and does its horrible spider walk for a few more inches before it stops.

I stand immobile, the thought of touching

anything in here makes me break out into a cold sweat; there will be others like that in here. Will they pounce as I hunt for the crowbar? What if they get upstairs? What if they creep into my bedroom?

My head starts to spin and I feel sick. Vivid memories of my childhood come back; banging on the door begging to be let out, standing on the steps, my legs aching because I was too scared to sit down.

For hours.

I close my eyes and breathe in deeply. I'm not a child anymore and I won't let her win.

I step towards the sideboard; Grandfather's wooden toolbox is in front of me underneath a lampshade and a pile of old *TV Times*. I push the magazines off and a cloud of dust billows upwards. I quickly pick up the lampshade and drop it to the floor. So far, so good. The toolbox lid is heavy and I have to use both hands to lift it open. I push the lid up and it falls back with a thunk and I jump back in case something nasty jumps out at me.

The inside is surprisingly neat and tidy; screwdrivers and hammers, spanners, handles with metal points, large metal files, even a hacksaw, all tucked in neatly, side by side. But nothing that looks like a crowbar.

I pick up the largest hammer, the wooden handle is worn smooth with use and the head is heavy. I can't bear to stay down here any longer. I heft the hammer in my hand, I'm sure it'll make short work of the dressing table drawer.

I turn around and step across the cellar, the huge spider has moved to the fifth step of the stairs. It's watching me. As I get closer it scuttles up the stairs

154

and disappears through the doorway. I gingerly walk up the stairs after it and can see through the doorway that it's run up the back of the dresser and is right in front of me. I stand in the doorway afraid that if I move it'll run – who knows where – up to my bedroom? In one swift movement I bring the hammer up and crash it onto the spider. I pull the hammer back and the spider is well and truly dead, several of its legs stuck to the hammer head. I notice that the back of the dresser now bears the imprint of the hammer head. I flick the remains of the spider onto the floor with the hammer head and then wipe it on the cellar steps.

I come out of the cellar backwards so that I can close the door and take the key from my pocket and lock it. I feel the tension leave me as I squeeze along the wall behind the dresser and I leave the dankness of the cellar behind me. Once out in the open I stand for a moment while my eyes adjust to the brightness of the room and then I realise that I've left the cellar light on.

I don't care; there's no way I'm going back down there.

I push the dresser back into place and go back upstairs to Mother's room.

'Where's the crowbar then?' She's sitting up in bed with the television remote control in her hand and has turned it on to her favourite quiz show.

'Couldn't find it.' I hold the hammer behind my back.

'I knew you wouldn't find it, it's in the cellar.' She gives a sly smile, 'I wouldn't expect you to go in there.'

155

'Why wouldn't I go in there?' I say as I move towards the bed.

'Because,' she says nastily, 'you're a coward. Just like your father.'

I stand for a moment looking down at her and realise that I hate her.

'Am I now?' I say.

And I pull back my arm and swing the hammer.

Chapter 15

Three swings of the hammer and the drawer is open. There's now a hole where the lock used to be and I pull it open easily with the tips of my fingers. Mother watches from her bed, immobile, a look of disbelief on her face. Even now she thought that I wouldn't do it, imagined that she still had some control over me.

The first things I see are boxes, or rather jewellery cases, old fashioned jewellery cases; velvet covered and worn smooth around the edges. I pick out the nearest one, a rounded, red square box with a tarnished gold hook keeping it closed. I unhook and open it and the glint of gold catches my eye, a delicate gold watch with diamonds set around a mother of pearl face, the wrist strap a delicate chain mail in gold. It speaks of cocktail parties, evening dresses, cigarettes in holders and long, elegant gloves. I can't imagine Mother ever wore it, I doubt it would even fit around her wrist.

'Very pretty, Mother.' I hold up the watch and the light dances and sparkles off the diamonds.

'It was your grandmother's,' she states flatly, glaring at me.

I try to imagine the austere, thin woman that I've seen in the photograph album wearing this watch.

'She wore it all the time when they were in India. Daddy, your Grandfather, was posted there just after the war. One long round of gin and parties by the sound of it.' Mother purses her lips disapprovingly. 'Before I was born, of course.'

I knew that Grandfather worked for the Foreign Office but I had no idea what he did. Of course they were young once, they weren't always old and thin and worn-out looking.

I wrap the watch around my wrist not expecting it to fit and am surprised when it does. I snap the clasp closed and hold my arm in the air to admire it.

'It's beautiful' I say. A feeling of loss hits me; the loss of a father I'll never know, the loss of grandparents that I can't remember. A feeling of what could have been had Mother been different, if Mother had loved me. If my grandparents had lived longer would she have been nicer to me? Would they have spoilt me and indulged me?

'It's not yours, you know. It's mine,' Mother snaps at me.

She has to spoil the moment. Always.

'But you're not wear going to wear it are you?' I snap back. 'It's wasted on you, you're not exactly going anywhere are you?'

'It's still mine though.'

'I think I'll just borrow it for a while, Mother. A watch like this deserves to be worn and shown off, not shut in a drawer.'

'It's valuable, you'll only go and lose it, or break it. Put it back in the box. Now.' There's a hint of panic in her voice but I ignore her and close the empty box and put it back into the drawer. I select another box and take it out; long and narrow this time. I open it and inside nestles a string of yellowing pearls. I study them for a while and then close the box and put it back in the drawer. I go through all of the boxes and there are lots of them; they take up half of the drawer. The other half is full of papers, some loose, some tied together in bundles. I deliberately don't look at them wanting to concentrate on one thing at a time.

All the boxes contain jewellery of some sort, a man's watch with a leather strap, assorted brooches, clip on earrings. I put them all back with the exception of one; a black leather box containing an emerald necklace. I put it on and admire myself in Mother's dressing table mirror; a delicate gold chain that sits just on my collar bone with a line of six emeralds set in gold edged in tiny diamonds. It brings out the green of my eyes and I decide that'll I keep this one too.

'Put it back, you can't wear that, you'll lose it.' Mother sounds and looks panicked. 'What if you lose it? It's not insured.'

I pay no attention to Mother and start to pull the loose papers out of the drawer and put them on the top of the dressing table. What I'm really interested in is the bundle of what looks like birthday cards and photographs tied with a shoelace.

'Don't look at them.' Mother has gone pale; she doesn't look very well.

'You know I'm going to look, Mother. I'd hardly go to the trouble of breaking the drawer open if I'm not going to look.'

'It won't make you feel any better, you know. Everything I did was to protect you.'

I pull the bundle out of the drawer and sit down on the end of her bed, just out of her reach. The knot in the shoelace is too tight to undo so I pick up Mother's nail scissors and snip it. The cards and photographs spill off my lap and onto the bed.

Birthday cards; a picture of a rabbit is on the first one I look at, *For a Daughter who is One Today!* inside the handwriting is small and neat, *To my darling Alison, with lots and lots of love from Daddy XXX.* I stare at it and pick up the next card, and then the next. Each one more or less the same, although the words differ slightly. Through a blur of tears, I look at each card, one for each year up until age five and then no more.

'You told me he didn't care.' I finally say in a hollow voice.

'He didn't. He left. You weren't even a year old.'

'But he sent me cards.'

Mother makes a noise of disgust, 'Birthday cards and presents, what good is that? I needed him here, not his money or his presents.'

'What presents? I never got any presents and you never gave me the cards. You told me you didn't know where he was.'

'Oh, I knew exactly where he was,' she snorts. 'He seemed to think he could have you but not me! I wasn't having that. He didn't want me so he wasn't having you either.'

'But he was my father, you should have let me see him. Where did he live?'

Mother clamps her lips together and shakes her head. 'I don't want to talk about him anymore.'

I know Mother; wild horses won't make her tell me if she doesn't want to. Why did he stop bothering? Why did he give up so easily? I wish I could remember him; I have absolutely no memory of him. I'd surely remember if he'd visited me, why didn't he?

'Why keep them?' I ask, 'Why keep them if you weren't going to give them to me? You threw the presents out so why keep the cards?'

A look I know well crosses her face; the *caught out* look and a memory of my fifth birthday leaps unbidden into my mind. A shiny, red bike with stabilisers and a little basket on the front to put my dolly in. The best birthday present that I ever got from Mother; I can't remember the ones before that but I remember the subsequent ones; gifts of clothes, knitted hats and scarves, pens and pencils, the occasional cheap toy if I was lucky. All things that I would have needed anyway but were given as presents by my tight-fisted mother.

'He sent me the bike, didn't he? For my fifth birthday? And you pretended it was from you.'

She sighs in a martyred way. 'Well, I couldn't afford fancy presents like that could I? I remember you were thrilled with it, so what's wrong with that?'

'You could have told me it was from him, given me the card as well.'

'You'd never met him, it would only have confused you.'

I look at Mother and wonder why she's so spiteful and full of hate. Did her parents make her like that or was she just born nasty? Something else I'll never know.

'Why keep the cards? Why not throw them out?'

'I'm not a monster you know. I thought maybe one day I'd give them to you.'

She pins a sad look on her face but I don't believe

her; more likely she saved them to torment me with. She says she's not a monster but she's not normal; there's something wrong with her, no one should be so bitter and hateful towards their own child.

I give up talking to her and pick up the bundle of photographs but they are of me and my grandparents; my grandmother holding me as a tiny baby in her arms on a sunny day, taken in our back garden. The awkward figure of my grandfather standing stiffly beside her, tight-lipped smiles on their faces. I've seen similar pictures in the photograph album. There are very few pictures of me in there; a couple of studio shots of me as a baby and the obligatory school photograph but no snaps of me growing up; no holiday snaps because we never had a holiday. I remember that Mother didn't even want the school photographs as she considered them a waste of money and I had to beg her to buy them. They stop at age eleven; hideously self-conscious by then I no longer wanted a mug shot of my spotty face above an unflattering school uniform.

There's no photograph of my father but I didn't expect one; Mother's hardly likely to keep a picture of a man she hated, is she? Old receipts, ancient out-of-date newspaper coupons, and then a yellowing, folded up sheet of paper clinging to the back of a photograph of my mother holding me as a tiny baby, the hint of a smile on her face. I pull the paper off it and open it out, carefully smoothing the creases flat. *Frogham Magistrates Court* is emblazoned across the top and I realise that I'm looking at a court order. The date is nearly two years after I was born and with a jolt I realise that my name is on there. As is my father's and Mother's. It's an injunction against my father stating that he's not allowed to contact my Mother or me in any way.

'What's this about?' I hold the order up to Mother.

'What does it say it is?' Mother sneers.

'It's an injunction.'

'That's right. To stop *him* pestering me.'

'What did he do? Did he threaten you?'

Mother laughs nastily. 'Well, that's what I told the court. But no, he didn't threaten me; too weak to do that. But he kept on, wanted to see you, thought he had *rights*.'

I stare at Mother in disbelief.

'You lied to a court to stop him from seeing me?'

'Served him right and the courts always side with the mother. He didn't want *me*, thought he could still have *you* and go back to *her*. So I made sure he couldn't. Shows how weak he was, didn't take him long to stop sending the cards and presents. He gave up after a few years.'

I continue to stare at Mother as it slowly dawns on me.

'He was married?'

'He couldn't be bothered,' she says spitefully. 'He didn't want you enough.'

'You haven't answered my question, was he married?'

'YES!' she shouts. 'He was married and he went back to her after our *fling* as he called it. She couldn't have children of her own but she thought she could have mine. *He* thought we could share custody. Well, I made sure that would never happen.' Mother smiles in satisfaction.

163

I feel dazed; my whole life she's told me that my father didn't want me, didn't care about me enough to contact me and I believed her. I made no attempt to find him and now it's too late; I'll never meet him. I feel devastated but I won't think about that now; I won't crumble in front of *her*. My life could have been so different. I could have had a father and a stepmother, a real family.

'Don't you have any pictures of him at all?' I gather up all of the paper and photographs into a pile.

'Pff! Why would I keep a picture of *him*?'

'Because he's my father, maybe I have a right to know what he looks like.'

'Right?' she bellows. 'Don't talk to me about rights! Who brought you up? Who's fed and clothed you all of your life?'

I open my mouth to reply but she shouts over me.

'And what thanks have I ever had for it? After all I've done for you, you treat me like a prisoner and rummage around my personal possessions. You're just like *him*, totally selfish.'

Mother's going to have an *episode*, the signs are all there; the raised shrill voice, the self-righteous certainty that she can do no wrong. I get up and walk out of her room and carry on straight down the stairs and into the kitchen. I take a bag for life shopping bag from the hook on the back of the kitchen door and go back upstairs. By the time I reach her bedroom she's shouting, ranting that will soon turn into unintelligible screaming about how ungrateful I am. I will most definitely not be staying around to listen to it.

I go into her room and sweep all the papers, cards

and photographs off the bed and into the carrier bag. I stand up and pause for a moment and then go to the broken drawer and pick out all of the jewellery boxes and drop those into the bag too. This causes a flurry of louder screaming from Mother; liar, thief, just like your father, are some of the things that I manage to pick out from the screeching.

She is screaming and glaring at me but I refuse to meet her eye and I come out of her room and close the door. I go along the landing into my bedroom and shove the bag into the bottom of the wardrobe and then quickly take the watch and necklace off and change into my running gear. I jog downstairs to the dining room and pull out one of the heavy dining chairs from the table and with immense effort I manhandle it up the stairs. I place the chair backwards in front of her bedroom door, tip it backwards and wedge the back underneath the handle. She won't be able to open it now. Mother can hear me doing this and it causes more screaming from her but I hold my tongue; I have nothing else to say to her. I'm going to have to think of a more permanent solution in case she tries to get downstairs again. Maybe a lock on her door, a padlock, possibly. I'll think about that later; the chair will stop her for now.

I'm going for a very long run and by the time I come back Mother will have exhausted herself and will be asleep.

I need peace and quiet to think.

I go back downstairs and just to be on the safe side I pick up the handset from the telephone holder and put it in my pocket. As I let myself out of the front door I can still hear Mother screaming but I think it's getting fainter; I think she's tiring herself out.

All the same, I'm thankful that we live in a detached house.

I run and run, trying to make sense of events. One part of me is devastated that I'll now never get the chance to meet my father but the other part is elated that he didn't abandon me deliberately; he tried but *she* stopped him.

I can't really mourn someone that I've never met but I mourn for what I might have had; what might have been. I knew Mother was vindictive but to deny a father the right to see his own child takes vindictiveness to a new level, even for Mother.

First thing on Monday I'll ring the solicitors and make an appointment to go in and see them. Perhaps my father has left me a letter or photographs? There must be some way I can find out about him, find out what he was like. I wonder if I have half-brothers and half-sisters and then realise that of course, that's not possible. How could I have siblings if I'm his next of kin and Mother said his wife couldn't have children. I could have aunts and uncles though, couldn't I? I could have other family apart from Mother. Maybe they could tell me about him. Perhaps I have relatives on my father's side who would welcome me; who would be a proper family to me.

I run past The Rise; it's warm for early May and the late afternoon sunshine has bought out dog walkers and joggers aplenty. I nod as I pass a familiar runner whom I often see on my nightly runs and a sudden bubble of happiness surges through me. It's so unexpected that I slow down to analyse why on earth I should feel happy.

What do I have to be happy about? My father has just died and I've never met him and now never will, that's hardly something to rejoice about, is it?

No, it's not. But I now know that he didn't abandon me, he *cared,* and that counts for something. I'm no longer the fat, unhappy downtrodden lump that I was, I'm fit, slim, young, and I have my whole life ahead of me.

I can do anything that I want. Mother no longer has control over me.

I realise that I haven't thought about Bella once since I opened the letter from the solicitor; haven't thought about the fact that I'm not cleaning there anymore.

But it doesn't matter, I decide, because things have a way of working out and I know, somehow, that things *will* work out for me.

Everything is going to be just fine.

Chapter 16

I wait for Doris at Joey's; I've managed to bag the window table so while I wait I people watch through the window as the world hurries by. Tuesday isn't our usual day for meeting up but I felt the need to talk to someone, I need to unburden myself before I explode. When I texted Doris asking her to meet I told her that my father had died but I didn't give any other details.

The café door bangs open hitting the wall and Doris stomps in. She comes straight over to me and bends over the chair and wraps her arms around me in a hug and holds me tight.

'Oh, mate, so sorry about your Dad.'

Tears spring to my eyes and I struggle to compose myself.

'You let it out, Al, let it go.' She thumps my back with her childlike hands and I surprise myself by bursting into tears.

We stay in this awkward position for several minutes while I sob hot, messy tears and my nose runs. When my sobs start to subside, Doris stands up and pats my hand.

'Sorry, mate, gotta stand up it's doing me fuckin' back in.' She puts her hand in the small of her back and leans back and stretches. 'Don't fink these shoes are helping neither.' She looks down at her feet, 'They

168

looked great on the shelf but they fuckin' kill.' She slips her feet out of them one at a time, stretches her toes and slips them back on, the back of both heels have plasters on that nearly cover the angry looking blisters.

'Got to break 'em in, nearly through the worst of it now.' She winces, 'Right, how about a cuppa? Fings always look better over a cuppa, as me mum says, or maybe she meant vodka.' Doris looks puzzled for a moment then goes on. 'Anyway, two teas coming up.' She clip-clops up to the counter in her four-inch-high, sling-back wedges.

I fumble around in my handbag and by the time she comes back I've blown my nose and composed myself and, surprisingly, I do feel a whole lot better. Unburdened.

'Joey's gonna bring 'em over.' Doris slides into the seat opposite me and wiggles around and I guess she's taking her shoes off again. 'Ah, that's better. Be sorry later when I've gotta put the fuckers back on.'

'Sorry for blubbing all over you.' I sniff.

'No worries, you gotta let it out or else you'll go nuts. Do you know when the funeral is? Or ave you got to sort it all out?'

The funeral? I hadn't even thought of the funeral; how self-centred am I? I hope I don't have to do it, I wouldn't have the first idea where to start. I'm sure the solicitor will tell me the arrangements when I have my meeting with him tomorrow, surely, he'll sort it out won't he? Come to think of it I don't even know the date my father actually died. I wonder who else will be there? Will I meet all of my father's side of the family? I drift off into a little daydream where I'm wearing a chic black dress and a hat with a veil and am introducing myself as my late father's mysterious daughter. I won't tell them I'm a cleaner, I decide, something more glamorous, an actress maybe. I could probably be an actress.

'Hmmph.' Doris coughs politely.

'Oh, sorry,' I say, 'lost in thought.'

'The funeral?' prompts Doris.

'Oh, yes, I don't know,' I admit. 'I don't know anything but hopefully I'll find out tomorrow when I see the solicitor.'

'So when was the last time you saw your dad?' asks Doris.

Joey interrupts us and deposits two cups of tea on the table and makes a swift exit when he sees the state of my face. I feel much better but must still look a wreck.

I contemplate Doris's question as I pick the teaspoon up and stir my tea; pointless as there's no sugar or milk in it. I really wanted coffee but don't say anything as I don't want to seem ungrateful. What version of the truth am I going to tell her? She knows my father isn't around but I've always been vague on the details.

'I've never met him.'

'What?' Doris gapes at me, 'What, never?'

'Nope. He cleared off, as Mother puts it, before I was born.'

'Christ, that's shit.' She shakes her head in disbelief.

'It is. I don't even know what he looks like.'

'What, you've never even seen a photo?'

'No. He could have passed me in the street and I

170

wouldn't have known him.'

Doris looks puzzled. 'What a bastard.'

I don't say anything and stir the tea that I don't want to drink.

'Sorry, Al. I shouldn't have said that.'

'It's okay,' I say sadly. 'No worse than what Mother's called him.'

Doris looks truly shocked now and I realise I've slipped up; the mother that I've described to her is a genteel, sweet little old lady who wouldn't hurt a fly.

'But of course she'd never use that word,' I go on. 'She calls him a cad and in her book that's the very worst thing she can say.'

'What's a cad?'

'A bastard. Same thing but more polite.'

'Oh. I see.' She says, even though she doesn't.

'So what I don't get is why didn't he contact you before he died?'

'I don't know,' I say. 'I've asked myself the same question many times.'

'You've never, y'know, been tempted to try and find him?'

'Thought about it. Should have done it but it's too late now isn't it?'

'Well, you weren't to know he was going to snuff it were you? And anyway,' she goes on, 'you'll find out all about him when you see this solicitor bloke.'

'Hopefully.'

'Do you fink,' Doris leans forward, looks around the café and lowers her voice, 'he's left you somefing?'

I plaster a puzzled look on my face.

'You know, a house or some money?'

171

'God,' I say as if I've only just realised what she's getting at, 'I haven't even thought about that. I don't know. Maybe.' An outright lie because of course I've wondered about it. I'm only human.

'You could be a millionaire.' Doris sits back and beams. 'You could tell old Ronnie to do one, no more cleaning houses for you.'

'Yeah, imagine her face.'

Doris and I laugh at the thought of Veronica's shock. I doubt somehow that my late father was a millionaire; in fact, I'm sure of it because if he was Mother would have found some way to rip him off. More than anything I want to know what he was like, what sort of man he was, what life he had and why he didn't come and find me. But if he has left me something that'll be a bonus won't it? Like I say, I'm only human and I certainly wouldn't turn my nose up at an inheritance.

'But, seriously Al, if you need some support, you know, at the funeral, I'll come wiv you.'

'That's so sweet of you, Doris. Thank you.' I smile. I'm touched, I really am. She's such a good friend.

But I wouldn't take her.

And I feel a bit bad even thinking it.

Because she's a bit low rent.

It's very quiet in the solicitors' waiting room, the tap of the secretary's keyboard the only sound. I've arrived way too early and as I cross and uncross my legs for the umpteenth time I wonder if I'm a bit overdressed. I didn't want to turn up in jeans and jumper. I thought somehow that I should mark the occasion, so I'm wearing the green dress that Bella

172

gave me, okay that I stole, with Grandmother's cocktail watch and her emerald necklace. I also have on a pair of new green suede court shoes with kitten heels. I didn't have shoes that did the dress justice, so I splashed out a hundred-and-twenty pounds on them. They're so worth it though, absolutely gorgeous and I can't stop admiring them. Every time I cross my legs I twist my calves this way and that; my legs look pretty good too. Anyway, Mother paid for the shoes, a very small compensation for Friday's horrific episode.

As expected she was fast asleep when I got home after my run, exhausted herself with her shenanigans. I'd been out running for nearly three hours, on and off. Running and thinking. Imagining different versions of my father, older than Mother, younger than Mother, handsome, ugly, fat, thin; you name it, I've thought of it.

The weekend passed quietly and no mention was made of Friday's episode; the broken drawer now pushed shut, the gaping hole where the lock should be the only reminder of what had occurred. Neither Mother nor I mentioned my father again. I cooked her meals and helped her to the bathroom and did all of the things that I've always done and even spoke to her quite normally. And she spoke to me, too, as if Friday's events had never happened. Only *please* and *thank you* and *would you like a cup of tea*, that sort of thing, no real conversation. But we never have conversations anyway; she used to tell me what to do or call me names but conversation? No, never.

I did make sure to put the back of the chair under her door handle so she can't get out and I think that'll do, actually. There's no way she can get the door open with the chair wedged there so I'm not going to bother with putting a lock or a padlock on.

As soon as nine o'clock came on Monday morning I was straight on the phone to the solicitors to make an appointment. The call was answered by Eunice, Mr Thompson's snooty sounding secretary who informed me that Mr Gerald was out of the office until Wednesday. After the crushing disappointment of having to wait two more days I spent the next five minutes asking her questions about my father which she refused to answer. She seemed to enjoy telling me that only Mr Gerald could tell me any of the details and that unfortunately I'd have to wait until Wednesday. I don't know how but somehow, I managed to rein my temper in as she graciously said that she would make me an appointment for today.

On arrival at the solicitors Eunice greeted me: late fifties, peroxide blonde hair with grey roots, hair-sprayed and coiffed into an elaborate beehive, thick pan stick make-up and matching orange lipstick which makes her teeth look yellow. Not what I was expecting at all. She was icily polite as I came in and spoke in such an affected, posh accent when she asked me to take a seat that it was all I could do not to laugh. I could feel her eyes on my back as I walked across to sit down. She didn't even try to hide the downward sweep of her eyes as she took in what I was wearing. I willed myself not to be so obvious and do the same to her although it was hard to miss the bold, sixties style black and white geometric shift dress she was wearing and the white, block heeled open toed sandals. Maybe she wore it all the first time around and kept it in her wardrobe for a sixties revival.

To stop myself from looking at my watch for the umpteenth time I pick up one of the many *Peoples Friend* magazines from the table and flick through the pages, staring at them unseeing. I expect Eunice keeps the office supplied with all of her old magazines. I will Mr Thompson to hurry up, I feel like I've been waiting forever but it's my own fault for being so early. I jump as the telephone on Eunice's desk chirrups; my nerves are in shreds and I need to get a grip. I've thought of every possible scenario for this meeting since I got the letter on Friday.

'Mr Gerald will see you now.' Eunice speaks so quietly out of the corner of her mouth that I only just catch what she's saying. I think she does it on purpose.

I chuck the magazine on the table, stand up and smooth my dress down, put my shoulders back and head towards Mr Gerald's office door which is behind Eunice's desk. Eunice doesn't lift her head as I strut by and I ignore the *please knock* sign on the door and fling it open and march straight in, nose in the air to show that I'm not happy at being kept waiting.

Even though I was early.

I was expecting Mr Gerald to be ancient, but like Eunice he surprises me, but in a much nicer way.

'Miss Travis, good to meet you. I'm Gerald Thompson.' The man getting up out of the chair and coming round to greet me is mid-thirties, very tall and as Doris would say, *well fit*. Short black hair tops a handsome, tanned face and when he smiles he reveals perfect white teeth. His hazel eyes openly appraise me but unlike Eunice I can tell that he likes what he sees.

I shake the proffered hand which is warm and dry and twice the size of mine.

'Hello,' I manage to mumble.

'First, may I start by offering my condolences.' He carries on and I nod and say nothing; for a moment I can't for the life of me remember why I'm here. Pathetic. A good-looking man is polite to me and I turn into a jabbering mess who forgets what she's supposed to be doing.

'Please, take a seat, Miss Travis.' He indicates the chair positioned in front of his desk as I stand gawping at him.

He goes back behind the desk and sits down and I sit down opposite him and cross my legs in what I hope is a seductive way. Hussy. I'm here to hear my father's last wishes and I'm flashing my legs for all I'm worth.

'Call me Alison,' I purr over the desk at him. God, I'll be licking my lips in a minute.

'Alison, I'm so sorry you've had to wait until now for an appointment but I've been away.'

I'm guessing skiing; the tan, the athletic build. He looks the action man type; he doesn't look the sort to laze around on a beach.

'Catalonia, water-skiing,' he says with a smile.

I nod and smile, as if I know all about it and go water skiing every week. I was nearly right; I bet he does ski but it's probably too late in the year for snow now.

'Anyhoo, to the business in hand. The sad news about your father must have been quite a shock as I understand you didn't have any contact with him?'

Anyhoo. Normally I find this intensely irritating and creepy but when he says it I don't mind. I actually find it very attractive.

'No, none at all, Gerald.'

He nods gravely and opens the beige folder in front of him; it's a good couple of inches thick, pages and pages of it. He brushes his hair back with his hand and I have the feeling that he's not sure where to start.

'Do you have a photograph of him? Of my father?'

'Um, no, I'm afraid we don't, although there may be some in his personal effects.'

I feel a flutter of excitement at the thought of what may be in my father's personal effects.

'Do you have them here?'

'No, not here, I'm afraid.' He shakes his head. 'They're being held at the home at the moment.'

'The home?'

'Yes. To give you some background, your late father's wife died fifteen years ago and after her death his health gradually deteriorated until he had to go into a nursing home. All of his personal possessions are being held in storage, awaiting collection.'

So he's been in a home all of these years and I never knew. All of the scenarios I've imagined him being in a home wasn't one of them. But why not? He'd be elderly, like Mother. I don't like the way he said they were being held in storage; makes it seem as if they've been there a long time.

'Oh. What I don't understand is why wasn't I told he was in a home?'

'Um. Well, the thing is, no one actually knew you existed until we went through his effects and found some paperwork with your name on it. Then we applied for your birth certificate and ascertained that the late Mr Patterson was your father.' Gerald clears his throat and looks down at the file.

'You mean I wasn't named as a beneficiary his will.'

'Um no. Mr Patterson didn't leave a will, he died intestate. His late wife had deposited her will with us which is why we were asked by the home to look into the matter of next of kin.'

Realisation slowly dawns. What an idiot I've been. He never left anything to me at all, never, ever, intended to contact me.

'When?'

'Sorry, when what?'

He doesn't want to tell me, he's stalling.

'WHEN did he die?'

Gerald clears his throat.

'Five months ago. He died five months ago.'

Chapter 17

Doris is waiting outside Moppers when I arrive on Friday morning to give in my timesheet. She looks at me expectantly.

'You alright, mate?'

'Yeah, I'm good. Veronica wants to see me so can I meet you at Joey's?'

She looks disappointed, she's desperate to know how I got on at the solicitors and I've already fobbed her off with *I don't want to talk about it* texts. She offered again to go to the funeral with me; supporting a friend and all that, she said.

'Yeah, course. I'll see if I can grab our usual table. What's old Ron want wiv you?'

'God knows.' I roll my eyes. 'I'll let you know later.'

I go inside and squeeze my way through the throng of cleaners and give my timesheet to Moira.

'Is there anyone in with her?' I nod in the direction of Veronica's closed door.

Moira looks up at me and sniffs.

'Don't think so. Give her a knock.'

I squeeze around Moira's desk and rap loudly on the door and go in without waiting for a reply.

Veronica is seated behind her desk and pauses mid-bite on a bacon and egg bap; she looks at me with annoyance.

'You're early.'

I ignore her and sit down in the chair opposite her.

'You wanted to see me?'

She places the bap carefully back in a greaseproof paper bag and scrunches the opening closed before replying.

'Yes. It's Rita, she's off sick again.'

'Really?'

'Yes. Not even back for a whole week and she's off again. It's too much.' She sighs in exasperation and looks longingly at her bacon and egg bap.

'What's wrong with her this time?'

'Oh, I don't know.' Veronica waves her hand dismissively. 'Same as last time I think, who knows? Anyway, the thing is I need to cover her shifts and what I need to know is can you do the Willoughby's shift again?'

Of course I can but I'm not going to make it too easy for her.

'Hmm, I'm not sure because I'll start to rely on it and then Rita'll come back and I'll be left in the lurch again.'

'I did offer you replacement shifts last time.'

I don't reply and look down at my handbag.

'But of course if you take the Willoughby's this time they'll be yours to keep. I can't be accommodating Rita's illnesses all of the time. When she's back she'll have to take one of the new clients.'

'Okay.' I say grudgingly, pretending not to be pleased.

'Could you take Petulia and Edith's shifts as well? They're not keen to do any extra.'

I'm about to ask who Petulia and Edith are when I

realise they're the pearls and twinset cleaners.

'No, sorry, no can do.' Veronica looks annoyed. 'I can't leave Mother on her own for too long. Not with the way she's deteriorated,' I hurriedly add, not wanting to upset Veronica too much.

'Okay. I'll ask around, see if anyone else wants some extra.' Her hand snakes towards the greaseproof bag so I take it I'm dismissed now and I pick my handbag to leave.

'Maybe try Doris,' I offer as I leave. Who knows how long Doris's boyfriend will keep his current job? She *might* be interested.

I walk slowly round to Joey's Cafe; I'm trying to decide whether to tell Doris the truth about my father.

The truth hurts; until I found out the truth I'd built up a nice little fantasy world where my father loved me and had been desperately wanting to see me for all these years but had been stopped by my evil Mother.

She had stopped him at first; but he obviously got over that and forgot all about me as he could easily have contacted me once I was eighteen. I keep telling myself that nothing's changed from how it's always been but of course it has. Now I know for sure; he didn't want me, or if he did he gave up at the first hurdle.

I haven't told Mother about the meeting and she hasn't asked but I have a feeling she knows, even though I've put on a happy face when I've seen her. I'm a pretty good actress, but not that good. Maybe she's afraid of what I'll do if she upsets me after the dressing table incident.

By the time I arrive at Joey's I still haven't decided if I'm going to tell the truth or not; I'll just play it by ear and see how it goes. Doris is ensconced in the corner and I don't bother ordering a drink but go straight over and flump down in the seat opposite her.

'What did the Ron want?'

'Rita's off sick again, she wants me to cover her shifts.'

'Bloody cheek! I 'ope you told her to fuck off.' Snorts Doris.

'I don't mind, said I'd do the Monday but I didn't want the other ones, apparently the pearl and twinsets didn't want them either.'

'Serves her right, she can't expect people to keep chopping and changing just 'cos Rita fancies a bit of time off.' Doris still hasn't forgiven Veronica for not finding her extra shifts when Charlie was sacked.

'Anyway,' she goes on, 'how did you get on at the solicitors?'

'Bit surreal really; I've missed the funeral, it was over a month ago.'

'No!' Doris looks shocked. 'That's terrible.'

'I know. Apparently, my father had a car accident several years ago and had been in a coma ever since so his affairs were in a bit of a jumble.'

'A coma? Poor fing.' Doris's eyes couldn't get any rounder.

'It wasn't helped by the fact that he'd been living in Australia for many years and had just come back to settle in England.' Absolute rubbish and I don't even know where it's all coming from but I'm warming to

182

my lies now and I can't seem to stop. Australia seems to be a theme with me as my imaginary boyfriend was Australian. Maybe I have a hidden yearning to go there; I haven't thought this story through, it's just come out, on the hoof or off the cuff or whatever the saying is.

'So had he been trying to trace you?'

'I think so. He'd only just arrived back in the UK when he had the accident in London and then he was in a coma and couldn't tell anyone about me. He's spent the last four years in a hospital in London and never regained consciousness.'

'Blimey.'

'They only found out about me because when he died a tracing directive was sent to the Solicitors Guild which generated a search of all the solicitors in the country. He'd lodged his will with Thompson's Solicitors and that's how they traced me.'

'Wow,' Doris says in admiration. 'That's like, so romantic.'

And so untrue. I feel a bit bad, all complete bullshit that just tripped off my tongue and I don't even know where it came from. Solicitors Guild? Tracing directive? I surprise myself sometimes. It helps that Doris isn't the brightest; she takes everything at face value and never questions what I tell her. I don't think that anyone else would believe me.

'It's just so tragic.' I shake my head sadly. 'I so nearly met Daddy. So near and yet so far.'

Doris has a strange look on her face and I think *Daddy* might have been a step too far. A bit too hammy. Strangely, though, I feel a bit better about it all. I think all the lying and story-telling has cheered me up a bit.

'Are you like, his only, whatchamacallit, heiress?'

'I think you mean beneficiary.'

'Yeah, that's it, beneficiary.'

'I am,' I admit. 'I'm his only living relative.'

'So come on, has he left you a load of money?'

'No, he hasn't.'

'Oh.' Doris looks disappointed.

'But he has left me a house.'

'A house? What, in Australia?'

I'm silent for a moment; this is the trouble with lies, they grow like Topsy and you have to keep inventing even more lies to stop it looking like you've lied in the first place. Exhausting, plus you have to have a good memory to remember all of the lies that you've already told.

'No, not in Australia, here in Frogham. It was rented out while he was in Australia and he was going to move back in when he came home.'

'Oh, I see. You lucky fing, your own house.'

And I would be very lucky indeed, if it were true. What I don't tell Doris is that he did have a house but it was sold to pay the fees for all of his years in the nursing home. After the solicitor's fees have been paid I've been left the princely sum of five hundred and forty-seven pounds and twenty-eight pence.

'Where is it? This house?'

See. Now I have to lie again and I need to be very careful that I don't say it's anywhere near one of Doris's many relatives.

'Oh, I'm not sure. The solicitor did give me the address but with everything that's happened I can't

184

remember.' I shake my head. 'My head's just been spinning with it all.'

'I bet. Are you going to sell it?'

'Not sure,' I say. 'Haven't really had a chance to take it all in yet. Bit of a shock.'

'I don't suppose you'll be able to move into it 'cos of your mum.'

'No, I couldn't leave Mother.' I arrange a concerned look on my face. 'Not with the way she's deteriorating.'

'So...' Doris begins hesitantly. 'If you wanted to rent it out again me and Charlie could rent it off you.'

Doris has a hopeful look on her face and I feel rotten for lying; I got carried away as usual and didn't know when to stop. I guess they're being evicted again for not paying their rent and are looking for somewhere else to live. If I really had a house I wouldn't rent it to them, they're nightmare tenants. Always in arrears with their rent and at the last place they rented Charlie attempted to decorate their bedroom in hot pink paint but then left it unfinished when he got fed up half way through. I'm surprised they manage to get anyone to rent to them, they must be black listed with most of the letting agents.

'No offence, Doris, but it's a four-bedroom house so the rent's probably going to be too high for you.' I wish I'd never started this stupid lie but I can't go back on it now.

'Not even at mate's rates? You wouldn't need to go through an agency or nuffin' with us being friends an everyfing. You wouldn't even have to pay tax on it.' She looks at me hopefully. 'And we could move in straight away,' she adds.

185

'If it was up to me I would,' I lie. 'But it's all tied up with probate and everything so I can't rent it out until that's all sorted.'

'Just a fort.' She shrugs, looking really disappointed and also a bit pissed off with me.

I need to stop this lying thing; I was really enjoying myself and got carried away and now I've upset Doris and I feel really bad about. If I really had a house I wouldn't rent it to her but that's not the point. I make a silent vow to myself not to tell any more lies and then quickly decide that it's pointless making a promise to myself that I won't keep.

No point in lying to myself is there? I'll be more careful in future with these stories I create. Perhaps I could plan them a bit more, not so off the cuff.

'So you don't know why he left it so long to look for you?'

'No. And now I'll never know so I'll just have to learn to live with that.'

'Yeah. Must be shit. My parents ain't up to much but they've always been there for me.' Doris slaps her hand across her mouth. 'Oops, sorry, me and my big mouf.'

'No worries,' I say with a smile. She looks smug, not sorry, but I probably deserve it and I wonder if she said it on purpose.

The minutes tick by as we sit in uncomfortable silence and Doris starts looking at her watch.

'Have you got to be somewhere?'

'Yeah, said I'd pop round me mum and dad's, haven't been round all week. Gonna ask'em if they can put me and Charlie up while we look for somewhere else to live.'

Ouch. A definite dig at me. I have upset her.

'Do you think they will?'

'Course they will, they're always saying we can move in anytime but they do me head in. Me and Charlie like to do our own fing and me mum fusses too much; tea on the table every night, soon as we take anyfing off it's washed and ironed. Drives me mad.'

See? Some people just don't know how lucky they are.

She pushes the chair back and stands up.

'You staying?'

'Yeah, I'll stop for a while, get myself a coffee.'

'Okay, see you next week.'

'Will do.'

Doris picks up her enormous PVC handbag, slings it over her shoulder and stomps away in her four-inch-high platform wedges. She doesn't look back as she goes out of the door. It's unusual for her to leave first; she can talk for England and it's normally me that suggests it's time to go. There was a definite coolness after I turned down her offer to rent my imaginary house and I feel she couldn't wait to get away. Perhaps I'm not such a good liar as I think and she knows I didn't want to rent it to her.

I go up and order a coffee and sit back down and wait for Joey to bring it over. I look at my watch to see that it's only half past eleven. At least I have Bella's to look forward to on Monday now that Rita is sick again. I've only missed going there for one week but it seems like forever.

Okay, that's another lie; I *did* go there on Monday but not to clean and not officially. I parked in the next street so Rita wouldn't spot my car and then walked around the corner to Bella's house. Rita's car was parked on the driveway where I always used to park. I felt absolute rage when I saw it; she didn't even thank me for looking after her clients when she was off sick and then she just comes back and takes over as if she's never been away.

It was just after ten o'clock and she always starts bang on nine thirty and has her set routine for cleaning so I knew she'd be upstairs doing the bedrooms for at least another half an hour. I quietly let myself in and went into the kitchen and I was in and out in five minutes so she never even knew I was there. I had my excuse ready just in case; I was going to say I'd popped in to see how she was getting on and to ask if she was better. I was going to say she'd left the front door open but as it turned out I'd didn't have to lie because she never came downstairs. It felt strange though; Rita upstairs doing the cleaning when it should have been me. But look how things have turned out; Rita's sick again and things are back to how they should be.

I have Monday to look forward to now but the weekend looms ahead of me; a weekend of tending to Mother, running, and nothing else. I have to collect my father's personal belongings from the nursing home but the burning inquisitiveness that I once had to know about him has vanished since I found out the truth from the solicitor. Honestly, I don't even know if I'll bother to collect them as I have no interest in him at all now; the visit to the solicitors was just another big let down. I might just ring the home and tell them to donate whatever's left to charity or throw it all in the bin.

But maybe the solicitors visit wasn't a total waste of time; I do have Gerald's mobile phone number. He made a big deal of giving it to me and said to call him anytime. I've thought about the way he said it over and over in my head and I don't think he meant to call him in an official way; I think he wanted me to call him in a personal way. I pull my mobile out of my bag and scroll through the contacts list.

My finger hovers over the screen; he wouldn't have given me his number if it was just business, would he? If I wasn't such an idiot I'd have given him my number and then he could have called *me*.

I stare at the screen pondering the long and lonely weekend ahead of me.

What the hell?

What's the worst that can happen?

I take a deep breath and press the call button.

Chapter 18

Bella's powder blue sports car is parked on the driveway when I arrive on Monday morning. This is a surprise and I experience a flutter of excitement in the pit of my stomach; she's never been at home when I've cleaned before, I'm finally going to meet her. There's no sign of Mr Justin-smarty-pants' car so I'm hopeful that he's not there.

I turn off the engine and sit in the car for a moment; there's no need to rush as I'm early anyway and also, I need to compose myself before I go in. I can't help feeling that everything is back on track. The weekend that loomed long and lonely on Friday turned out to be quite different from normal and I don't know why I was so nervous about ringing Gerald because as soon as he heard my name he couldn't wait to ask me out to dinner on Saturday night.

Of course I had nothing suitable to wear so I had to use Mother's card to buy myself a new dress. And shoes, because of course none of mine went with the dress. And then there was a really nice necklace that matched the dress so I bought that too. I didn't want to wear the emeralds again because I wore them the first time we met and I think Gerald's the sort who would *notice*.

I didn't tell Mother I had a date, there's no need

for her to know and she'd only have tried to make me feel bad and spoil it for me. She's been very quiet for the last few days, says she's got a headache and doesn't feel right. I don't know whether she's playing for sympathy or not although she did look a bit pale and washed out. Although she's eating everything that I cook for her so I'm inclined to think she's putting it on.

I didn't want Gerald coming into the house so I kept looking out of the window and as soon as I saw his car I went out to meet him. He seemed a bit surprised so I had to tell him about Mother. Not the whole truth obviously; I said that she was ill, which is true, and that the carers are in and I'd let myself out as I didn't want to disturb them. I thought it through this time; if I lied and pretended I didn't live with Mother he might want to come in. I couldn't have that, I can't imagine Gerald would be very impressed with the seventies furniture and decoration in here; that's just beyond embarrassing.

Anyway, he took me to a very nice Italian restaurant, all dim lighting with red candles stuck in Chianti bottles and Italian waiters who probably aren't Italian at all. We made a good-looking couple even though I say it myself. Gerald had on a pair of navy chinos with a crisp white shirt finished off with a beige linen jacket. He smelled gorgeous too, a subtle and probably very expensive not-in-your-face aftershave. I was wearing my new dress and shoes and I'm not being big headed when I say I looked pretty good.

When I was getting ready to go out I was fretting a bit; what was I going to talk about, what if he asked me about my job? Obviously, I wasn't going to tell him I'm cleaner but I couldn't decide what I was going to be because every time I decided on something I was afraid he'd ask me questions about it. In the end I decided I'd just wing it and as it turned out I needn't have worried.

Gerald likes to talk. About himself. I could tell you every detail about his recent water-skiing holiday, even the names of the people he went with. His house, I could describe that in minute detail and I even know much he paid for it, *absolute bargain*, according to him.

He did ask me where I worked and on the spur of the moment I said I was a freelance cookery writer. *Wow, how interesting*, was his response and that was it, straight back onto the important topic of conversation - him. So I didn't need to worry at all, I could have told no end of lies and he didn't even need to believe me because he was too busy listening to the sound of his own voice.

That's not to say I didn't have a nice evening though, my lasagne was very nice and I enjoyed the admiring looks from Gerald. And the waiters. When it came to the bill I wasn't sure of the etiquette; it's ten years since I've been on a date and I was still at school and everyone paid their own way. Gerald clicked his fingers importantly and asked for the bill. When it came he made a big deal of getting his gold American Express card out and I thought; *go on then, I've listened to you talking all night so the least you can do is pay for the meal.*

I know that I'm not used to spending time with people, apart from Doris and Mrs Forsyth, and I don't sit *talking* with people so maybe I expect too much. Because although I was the listener (because I couldn't get a word in) I was exhausted. Sounds stupid doesn't it? By the end of the evening I was worn out with listening to him. He jumped from one subject to the other and frankly, I couldn't keep up and I gave up trying. Which didn't matter because as long as I made the appropriate interested noises and fascinated expressions that's all that was required.

Anyway, I don't think he expected me to pay and he made a big show of giving an over generous tip to the waiters who'd been fawning over him all night. It's his favourite *go to Italian* so they obviously know he's a big tipper but what I saw and he didn't – because he was too busy talking – is that those fawning waiters were making faces at each other behind his back, rolling their eyes about him and sniggering.

We came outside and it was a lovely warm evening, a romantic sort of evening. We got into his car and he suggested that we go back to his place for a *nightcap* but I think he was expecting me to spend the night with him. Like I say, it's been a long time since I've been on a date and maybe that's expected now; sort of payment for the meal. I said no and that I had to get back to Mother and I think he was surprised and a bit annoyed, although he tried to hide it. I just wasn't feeling it. I don't fancy him; although I was tempted to have sex with him just to see if he could actually shut up. Unless he talks all the way through that as well.

When we got to my house he pulled up outside and to my amazement he asked me out again. I didn't think he'd bother after I turned him down but then I realised that he thinks I'm playing hard to get. I didn't want to commit myself so I told him I was away on business for a few days but I'd give him a call when I got back. He didn't even ask anything about where I was going; talk about self-obsessed.

So he leaned in for a kiss, which I allowed, and it was okay; his breath was bit garlicky from the Italian meal but I expect mine was too. He said how much he'd enjoyed the evening and launched into a great big long diatribe about how and when he'd discovered his *go to Italian* and I had to stop myself from shouting *shut up! For God's sake give your mouth a rest.*

When he paused for a nanosecond to draw breath I used the opportunity to open the car door and make my escape.

So. That was then and this is now; I look at my watch and I'm only five minutes early now so I think I'll go in. I've decided that I'm not going to knock even though Bella's car is on the drive, it's just awkward knocking and waiting for an answer. I'm going to go in and act as if it's just a normal cleaning day, which it is, except Bella's there.

I get my key out ready, grab my cleaning kit and get out of the car. A quick check of the upstairs curtains confirms they're open so she's not still in bed. I quietly let myself in the front door, put my cleaning kit in front of me on the floor and then gently close the door. Normal closing; not too loud and not too quiet as if I'm trying to sneak in, just normal.

I stand and listen for a moment. I can hear talking

from upstairs, a woman's voice which I guess is Bella's but she doesn't sound at all like I thought she would.

I expected Bella to have a soft, measured, well-spoken voice. The voice coming from upstairs is shrill, strident and screeching, almost shouting.

I quietly move to the bottom of the stairs so I can hear.

...it must be bad or else you wouldn't have been suspended.' There's silence after she's spoken so I'm guessing she's on the phone. It's very quiet and I can hear her pacing around up there and I hope she doesn't look down the stairs otherwise she'll see my cleaning kit in front of the door.

I contemplate quickly moving it when the sound of her voice stops me and this time she *is* shouting.

'Don't lie to me! Don't fucking lie! They found it on your laptop Justin and only you use it so you can't blame it on anyone else.'

The cleaning kit will have to wait; I daren't move now. I feel a small thrill of satisfaction; it sounds as if my plan has worked and Mr Justin-smarty-pants has been caught out. I hear the thud of footsteps crossing the landing and then more shouting.

'Were you looking at it when I was here? When you told me you were working in your study, were you really looking at that filth?'

Silence, then:

'You do know, so stop lying. Is it children? Please tell me it's not children!'

The shout turns into a scream on the last word and she must have hurled the phone across the room as I hear the sound of something hitting the wall. I stand frozen to the spot and listen to Bella crying; great heaving sobs that reverberate down the stairs. I should feel bad; I *do* feel bad for Bella's distress but she'll get over it, plenty more fish in the sea and all that. I'm actually surprised how well it's all worked out, it's all gone to plan. Because no matter how well you plan and execute something you never know if it'll work when it comes to the crunch; it wasn't as if I could rehearse it or anything. As for Justin it serves him right, talk your way out of that one, *strangefruit.*

I remain standing at the bottom on the stairs in an agony of indecision. Can I get to the front door unseen and pretend I've just arrived? I hover uncertainly and then hear the bang of a door slamming upstairs; whatever room Bella's in she's shut the door. I take my opportunity and skip over to the front door, open it and then close it loudly.

'Helloo,' I shout out cheerily. 'Anyone home?'

Silence.

I open and shut the door again, a bit louder this time, and after a moment there's the definite sound of an upstairs door being opened.

'Hello?' Bella's hesitant voice drifts down the stairs.

'Hello!' I bellow. 'It's Alison, the cleaner.'

Silence for a moment and then a blonde head pops around the top of the banister rail at the top of the stairs.

'Sorry, I forgot you were coming.'

Her hair is loose so I can't see her face as she's hiding behind it and won't look at me face on.

'That's okay, I'll start in the kitchen as usual.'

The blonde hair disappears and then the sound of

her bedroom door closing.

Bit rude, if I'm honest, but I'll forgive her this once as she's obviously having a stressful time.

I bend down and slip my shoe covers on, collect my cloths and cleaners and pad out to the kitchen. She'll have to come out of her room sooner or later and then I'll get to meet her properly. I'm glad that I made the effort and washed my hair this morning; a part of me must have known that I was going to meet her today. I've still got the awful Moppers tabard on – Veronica insisted on giving me a smaller size to wear - but my leggings and t-shirt fit me now and they're not Foodco specials, they're nice expensive ones from Helicon Sports.

The kitchen worktops aren't quite as full as usual of dirty dishes and I realise that Justin must have been gone for a few days as it's mostly cereal bowls and small plates with crumbs on. It looks like Bella's been living on cereal and toast so Justin must have been the chef. Another thing we have in common; we're both crap cooks. I hum happily as I load the dishwasher and clean the kitchen and wonder if Justin will get the sack. Would serve him right for mocking people less fortunate than himself.

Kitchen cleaned, I decide to change my normal routine and do the lounge next, give Bella a bit more time to pull herself together. I whiz around dusting the lounge and then get the vacuum cleaner out from the cupboard under the stairs and vacuum the entire ground floor. I clean the downstairs toilet and then mop the kitchen floor.

When I've finished I stand at the bottom of the stairs unsure what to do. I thought Bella would have come down by now; should I just go upstairs and carry on as usual? I think I should, after all Bella doesn't know that I know. Decision made I pick up the vacuum cleaner and walk upstairs a bit noisily to get her attention. I dust the skirting boards on the landing and am wiping down the banisters when I hear the creak of her bedroom door opening. Her hair is tied back in a neat chignon and she's applied some make-up. I'm impressed; you'd never even know she'd been crying.

'Hi,' I say with a smile as I look up from my dusting.

'Hi. I don't think we've met before, I'm Bella.' She puts her hand out.

'Hi Bella, I'm Alison.' I take her hand and shake it gently.

'I don't want to get in your way so I'll go downstairs and you carry on as normal.'

I move aside to let her down the stairs and watch her; shoulders back, head held high.

I go into their bedroom and the lack of his clothes on the floor confirms that he hasn't been here for a few days. As I pick Bella's dirty washing up I notice that she's left her mobile phone on the dressing table. It's next to a smashed landline handset which I guess is the one I heard being hurled against the wall.

I step over to the mobile phone and look at it for a moment and then pick it up, keeping an eye on the bedroom door at the same time. The phone's locked and requires a code to unlock it. I tap in 1,2,3,4,5 and 6 but it doesn't work. On a hunch I tap in Bella's date of birth and I'm in, I scroll straight to messages and tap on Justin. I step over and shut the bedroom door and quickly read through the latest ones.

Justin: Honestly babe, I haven't done anything wrong. Someone else must have put stuff on there.

Bella: How? It's your laptop, no one has access to it but you.

Justin: I don't know. I've hired an IT expert to look into it for me. I'm not just going to roll over and give in and lose my job over it.

Bella: Well you're hardly going to admit it are you?

Justin: I'm not going to keep telling you it wasn't me. I thought we knew each other but if you believe this of me then you don't know me at all. I've given you space but I'm not going to keep apologising for something I haven't done. It's bad enough that I've been suspended.

Bella: I need to think about it.

Justin: I wouldn't need time to think about it if you were accused of something.

Bella: I'll call you later.

I place the phone back carefully where it was and mull it over. She's weakening, I'm pretty sure she's going to give in and have him back.

That simply cannot happen.

Why? The rational side of me asks, why is so important to me that Justin loses his job and loses Bella as well?

Because he has to pay; for all of the years I've been laughed at, sneered at and made the butt of other people's jokes. Okay, it wasn't him but I can hardly track down every single person who's made me feel like shit and punish them, can I? So, he can take the punishment for all of them.

I jump at the sound of the bedroom door being opened. Bella pops her head into the room.

'Just looking for my phone, not sure where I left it.'

I pretend to look around and spot it on the dressing table.

'There it is.'

Bella comes in and picks it up and walks back towards the door. She's going to ring him and give in; I can feel it. I need to stop her.

'Bella?' I call as she disappears through the doorway.

'Yes?' She turns around and I sense a hint of annoyance from her that I'm bothering her.

'Is it okay to clean the study today?'

'Yes, of course.' She seems puzzled by my question.

'Okay.' I reach down and drag the vacuum towards the en-suite. 'Just checking, because Mr Willoughby doesn't like me cleaning it usually.'

'Sorry?' She looks totally confused now.

'When he's working in there. He doesn't like me in there when he's here so I just wanted to be sure.'

'But he's never here. Well, maybe just the odd time.'

'Oh, dear. I hope I haven't spoken out of turn.'

'What do you mean?' Bella's voice is less friendly now.

'I'm sorry but he's nearly always here when I clean. More often than not. He got quite angry the first time I went in there when he was here; said he didn't pay cleaners to snoop on him.'

I stand still and watch her face as the tumblers fall into position; the dawning realisation that he's a liar. Her reaction surprises me though, I'd expected tears.

'Alison,' she says shakily, 'why don't you have a break and come downstairs and have a coffee?'

'That…' I place the vacuum hose back on the floor. 'Would be lovely.'

I don't think she'll be taking him back now.

Chapter 19

'So Justin was here more often than not?'

We're seated at the kitchen table drinking coffee that Bella's just made. I've only been offered instant, not the good stuff that comes out of the thousand-pound coffee maker sitting on the worktop. In coffee hierarchy cleaners obviously don't merit the good stuff.

She tries to say it casually, as if what she's saying isn't important but she doesn't fool me; her mind must be in a whirl. She's a cool one that's for sure; when I arrived, she was crying hysterically and screaming at Justin and now she's calmly pretending to make small talk with me so she can find out what he's been up to.

I make her wait and delay my answer by slowly twirling my cup around on the chunky table top that exactly matches the worktops, whilst biting my lip to make her think I'm not sure if I should tell her or not.

'Most of the time,' I blurt out and then immediately clap my hand over my mouth as if to take back what I've just said. 'Gosh, I haven't said something I shouldn't have, have I?' Honestly, I deserve an Oscar.

'No, no, of course not.' Bella laughs unconvincingly. 'I just need to have a word with him; he gets so stressed about work and it's not fair if he's rude to you. You're only trying to do your job.'

'Mmm.' I take a sip of my coffee, which actually, is pretty vile; bitter and tasteless and she's put milk in it even though I don't take it. She never asked how I liked it, just assumed. Or didn't care. She poured the water into the cup while the kettle was still boiling which has tainted it. But it's good enough for the cleaner, obviously. I notice she hasn't touched her own.

'I know how stressed people get over work, especially when it's top secret. You have to be so careful these days.' I say quietly.

Bella gives a tight-lipped smile and speaks through gritted teeth. 'Yes, he does have a very demanding job.'

'That's what I thought.' I take another sip of coffee, God it's vile. 'Alison, I said to myself, Mr Willoughby can't have just anyone walk into his study and look at the screen when his job is so confidential. He wouldn't want to be shutting his laptop every five minutes just so you could do a bit of dusting, would he? I quite understand that he didn't want me in there and shouted at me. He obviously didn't want me seeing something that I shouldn't.'

I take a sly look from under my eyelashes at Bella to see that she's got the message and I pick up my cup again and pretend to concentrate on my coffee. Get out of that one smarty-pants Willoughby. Bella keeps her face impassive, only the slight flaring of her nostrils betraying her feelings. See, there's always a tell-tale sign if you know where to look; mine's holding my breath which I think is better because no one can see that I'm doing it. As long as I don't hold it too long, obviously. I do admire Bella, she still looks stunning even after the crying and screaming; she has absolutely flawless skin even without any make-up.

'Do you have many other people that you clean for, Alison?' She's looking at me with a polite smile and the sudden change of subject makes me think that she's heard all she needed to. I can sense that any minute the coffee cups will be whisked away and I'll be banished back upstairs again. She's found out what she wanted to know and my company is no longer required. So now we'll have a few minutes of chit chat to throw me off the scent and I'll be dismissed to resume my skivvying. Why am I surprised? Did I think we'd become friends? I suppose I did, I'd sort of hoped she might confide in me; maybe break down in floods of tears and use me as a shoulder to cry on. I could have been a sympathetic listener too, I'd have agreed with her about what a total bastard Justin is. Realistically, I knew that wasn't going to happen but you can't stop yourself from hoping.

'Not too many,' I say. 'I'm fitting it around my Open University course so I have to leave plenty of time for studying. I don't want to mess up getting my degree.'

This is her cue to ask me what I'm studying, twentieth century literature, I'd decided, as I've read lots of books so can pretty much wing it. I haven't seen any books in this house, just glossy magazines so I'm taking a guess that Bella's not a reader and is unlikely to catch me out. I want her to know that I'm not your average lowly cleaner, that I'm on her level. Well, above it actually, because she doesn't have a degree and her A levels are worse than mine.

But she doesn't bat an eyelid when I say it and doesn't ask and actually, I don't think she even listened to my answer. I can't help feeling a bit disappointed in her, she could have shown some interest if only to be polite. But I should forgive her I suppose; she has just found out her boyfriend's addicted to porn and has been viewing it at every opportunity on his laptop. She then surprises me totally by what she says next.

'My grandparents live near you.'

'Do they?' I say in surprise. How on earth would Bella know where I live?

'You live at Duck Pond Lane, don't you? My Nan and Grandad live at number one.'

Ah, the ancient crones who've been there forever. I'm surprised that her grandparents live in a terraced house; I'd expected better, thought she came from a classier background. They could be the poor side of the family I suppose; maybe one of her parents married up.

'I pop in and see them most weeks and I've seen you when I've visited them, you live in that huge, cream, stone house, don't you?'

She's noticed me! Bella has actually noticed me. I feel elated and I experience a rush of pride that we live in a detached house and not one of the tiny terraced cottages. From the outside our house looks quite grand and imposing, and even though a little run down there's no hint of the ghastly seventies brown and orange interior. This must surely be fate; a sign of yet another connection between us. Maybe I was too quick to dismiss the possibility of becoming friends.

'I do,' I say with enthusiasm and maybe putting on a slightly posher accent. 'I often see your grandparents pottering around in their front garden. I sometimes stop and have a chat with them if I'm passing.' A complete lie; I have attempted to wave to them on occasion but they just stand and stare miserably at me. They're so decrepit they're most likely senile so Bella's hardly going to know I'm lying, is she? She doesn't look disbelieving so I think I've got away with it.

'I've often seen you going out running when I've been visiting.'

'Yes, I go out most evenings for a run, it helps me de-stress, what with my coursework and looking after Mother.'

I feel I need to tell her this to explain why I'm a cleaner and I'm still studying for a degree at my age. Not that she knows how old I am but I'm obviously not eighteen.

'Mother can be quite difficult,' I lower my voice and continue in a confiding tone, 'what with her dementia getting worse every day. But of course, I'd never let her go into a home. That would be unthinkable.'

'With your physical job and all that running you must be super fit.' She smiles her tight-lipped smile again which never reaches her eyes and I realise that she's not really interested at all. Although she's obviously noticed that I'm in good shape; I think we're pretty much the same size now. I decide to take the compliment and enjoy it even though it was said in a half-hearted way; make the most of it. I'm still basking in it when she ruins it. Absolutely ruins it.

'It's hard to believe you were once so, erm, big. I didn't believe my Nan when she told me you were the same person - I honestly thought you had a sister. You look *so* different.'

She means it as a compliment, she thinks I should be flattered and has no way of knowing that she's spoilt everything.

Everything.

In Bella's eyes I'll always be the giant fat person who managed to lose weight; that's all I'll ever be. She'll never think of me as her equal now. I'm the fat girl who went on a diet and lost loads of blubber but one day, probably not too far in the future, I'll explode and put it all back on again. And more.

'Whatever diet you've used you should market it.' Is that the hint of a sneer I can see? As in *you're a big fat pig and always will be inside.*

Shut up.

Just shut up.

How can she prattle on about my weight when she's just discovered her partner is a porn addict? I stretch my mouth into the semblance of a smile and get up from the chair.

'Thanks for the coffee but I must get on.'

'Yes of course,' she says with disinterest. 'Time's money and all that.' I can tell from the faraway look in her eyes that I'm forgotten already and she's back to thinking about Justin. She gets up from the table and wanders out of the kitchen and into the lounge and I hear the sound of the lounge door closing. She does this all without speaking another word to me.

Feeling dismissed I pick up the cups from the table and carry them over to the dishwasher. Her cup is still full, she never even took one sip from it. I have an urge to hurl the cup at the wall and imagine it hitting the pristine paintwork in a crash of broken china and coffee. I take a deep breath and carefully pour the contents of the cups into the sink. I pick the discarded spoon up from the worktop where Bella tossed it when she'd finished making the coffee and I wipe the coffee stain away from underneath it with the dishcloth. It's a nice spoon; probably really expensive, shiny, sleek and elegant, like Bella actually. I hold the bowl of it in one hand and the handle in the other and twist it roughly. Not so nice now, slightly bent. I twist it a bit more; definitely bent now. I walk over to the bin and press the button on it and the lid flips up. I launch the spoon into the bin with all of the force I can muster and it lands with a thud on a mush of teabags and discarded magazines.

I turn around and study the kitchen; it's beautiful, a dream kitchen that must have cost a king's ransom and anyone would love to have a kitchen like this but Bella and Justin can't even be bothered to look after it, they treat it with contempt. They don't appreciate all that they have because they know no different. Born lucky, that's what they are; money, good looks and no doubt they both have doting parents who lavish love and affection on them and gave them idyllic childhoods and the very best of everything. I'm quite sure that Justin will manage to hang onto his highly paid job and wriggle his way out of the *porn on a works laptop charge* and it'll all just be a minor blip in his brilliant career. Probably be turned into an amusing after dinner anecdote in the future. Bella, of course, will have him back when he's done the required amount of grovelling and their perfect life will be restored. She knows which side her meal ticket's buttered on that's for sure.

Okay, Justin didn't actually do anything wrong, it was me, but it just proves that some people are non-stick, slippery like Teflon so that nothing bad or horrible sticks to them. I've been quite restrained really; I could have used his credit card details to access a child porn website and even *he* would *never* have recovered from that. I didn't do that because I couldn't stomach it myself, I couldn't even bear to search online for it.

How strange that something that seemed so important to me suddenly seems such a waste of time and energy. An hour ago, my obsession with Bella – and I can see now that it was an obsession – took over my every waking moment. It spurred me on to lose weight and change my life, and for that I'm thankful. But she hasn't actually done anything to help me, it was all in my mind and I'm struggling now to understand what I thought was going to happen. Did I honestly imagine that Bella and I would become friends?

I really don't know what I was thinking; I've had too many years of just me and Mother when I should have been having a life and maybe I've gone a bit mad. I can blame Mother all I like but I *allowed* her to treat me like a skivvy and belittle me for all of those years. I could have stood up to her sooner if I hadn't been so feeble. I allowed her to dominate me because I felt weak but I'm different now; I've changed and I don't need someone to idolise or to use as my lucky charm. I don't need Bella anymore.

There are some things I've done that I maybe shouldn't have but I'm not going to waste time worrying about them now; I can't change them and there's no harm done. Hopefully. Anyway, Justin deserved bringing down to earth even if it's only for a short while.

I rinse the sink and then take a last look around the kitchen before I go back upstairs to finish the cleaning. As I pass the closed lounge door I can hear the murmur of Bella's voice; she's talking to someone on the phone. Most likely Justin.

I realise with a feeling of incredulity that I don't care anymore if she takes him back or not, although I'm sure she will. I've completely lost interest in Bella, almost as quickly as I became obsessed with her. I climb the stairs and maybe I'm imagining it but I feel lighter, as if I've been set free. I go into their bedroom and resume picking up the discarded clothes from the floor.

Why did I ever think Bella was so special? Yes, she's beautiful, but she's also lazy and content to let someone else pick up her dirty knickers and clear up her mess, which makes her slightly grubby in my opinion. Pride wouldn't let me allow someone to handle my soiled underwear. She has a good job but I know from her emails that her looks certainly helped her, she didn't get there on talent or merit alone. It's quite possible that she slept her way up the career ladder and not just with anyone, but with her ex-boss serial killer, the Frogham Throttler, too.

Is she a nice person? I don't think she is; it didn't take a lot to turn her against her partner. Once the taint of porn touched Justin she was ready to jettison him and believe the worst of him which shows that she has no loyalty.

I'm not a nice person either so I have no right to judge but if I'm going to idolise someone surely they should be better than me, and she's not. I know that I haven't treated Mother very well lately; I've stolen from her and made her a prisoner in her own home but that's no different to the way she's treated me. She's stolen ten years of my life and I became a prisoner trapped in an obese body. Not totally her fault; she didn't actually force the food down my throat but she contributed to making me so miserable that my only solace was food.

No, I don't feel bad about the way I've treated her; I still feed her and look after her and her life hasn't really changed, well apart from me not letting her have a stair lift to come downstairs. She only has herself to blame because she brought me up and I learned from the best; I'm the way I am because of her.

I go into the bathroom and throw my armful of dirty washing into the laundry hamper. I clean the scummy ring from around the bath and scrub the sinks and toilet until they're gleaming. I have a little chuckle to myself as I remember using Justin's flashy electric toothbrush to clean the toilet bowl. Yes, extremely childish but immensely satisfying as well. The burning hatred that I felt for Justin is starting to diminish. Not enough to make me regret what I've done. I know he'll be fine but he needed teaching a lesson. I'm sure no long-term harm has been done; his charmed, lucky life will continue unchanged after the porn smudge on his copybook.

Bathroom finished I go back into the bedroom and remake the bed and vacuum the carpet. Into the dressing room where there are clothes hanging out of the wardrobes and the doors are flung wide. I tuck them back inside and re-hang the dresses trailing from the hangers and close the doors so that the room looks tidy. I know now that I'll never wear the green dress again; it somehow feels tainted and although it's by an expensive designer and probably cost a fortune, if I'm being honest it looks slightly cheap. Maybe I'll give it to Doris, she'd love it although she'll never believe it's real designer; she'll think it's a knock off from the market.

I dust and clean the rest of the rooms and I know it'll be the last time because I'm saying goodbye to this house, I'm going to request that someone else takes this house on until Rita comes back to work.

The scales have truly fallen from my eyes.

I'm done here.

Chapter 20

As I pull the car into Duck Pond Lane I don't realise straight away that there's a police car parked outside my house. My mind is preoccupied with the events of the last five months and the changes that I've made. I've driven home from Bella's house on autopilot and part of me feels a little sad that she's no longer going to dominate my life. I'm also feeling embarrassed with myself for having what amounts to a crush on another woman. Thank God I never confided my feelings to anyone else. If Doris had been a different sort of person I might well have felt the need to unburden myself. I pull the handbrake on and am congratulating myself on keeping my mouth firmly shut when I notice that there's a police car parked in front of me.

I've pulled up right behind it without even realising. Trivial thoughts of embarrassing myself are replaced by panicked thoughts as to why the police are here. They could be visiting anyone, I tell myself. Just because they're parked outside my house doesn't mean they've come to see me, there are other people who live in the street and they could be visiting any one of them.

Yes. That'll be it; I can see that there's no one in the car so they must be visiting someone else in the street. I pick up my bag from the passenger seat with a feeling of relief which quickly disappears when I see that a tall, dark suited man and a uniformed police woman are walking up the path to my front door.

I sit with my bag on my lap for a moment and try to think rationally to quell my mounting panic. It can't be about Justin's laptop; the police aren't that quick surely? No, I've only just left Bella's house so it can't possibly be because of that. Even if Justin has got a posh IT friend and an expensive lawyer there hasn't been time for him to do anything yet. I know money talks but it doesn't talk that quickly.

I take a deep breath in through my nose and exhale slowly through my mouth. I do this several times. No. It must be something unrelated, a pure coincidence. All I have to do is not panic and in the unlikely event it's something to do with Justin I'll just have to act a bit thick. Acting a bit thick used to be one of my specialities, people almost expect it when you're supersize; your body is enormous therefore your brain must be tiny. I'm not sure how well it'll work now I'm normal size but it's definitely worth a try.

A horrible thought pops into my head; could Mother have somehow managed to call the police? Could she have managed to get down the stairs and phone them? She managed to drag herself downstairs once before. Or could she have attracted a neighbour's attention from her bedroom window?

Keep calm and think. No. It's not possible. I wedged the dining room chair firmly under the door handle of her room when I left this morning and her bedroom window is mostly blocked by her dressing table. Even in the unlikely event that she managed to pull herself up and reach the window no one would hear her shouting through the double glazing. Even if someone in the street looked up by chance and saw her now that I've put it about that's she got dementia they'd just think she was doollally.

So, it must be something else but I have no idea what. I could drive off and wait to come home until they've gone because they haven't noticed me yet. This is momentarily appealing due to my natural cowardice but I know I'm only delaying it and I'll just be waiting for them to come back so I won't have gained anything except a sleepless night. No, the only way to find out is to man up and get out of the car.

I slowly open the car door and clamber out, lock the door and then force myself to walk unhurriedly across the pavement and into the front garden and up the path. The policewoman has her finger pressed on the bell and seems to be leaving it there for a very long time, I can hear the faint chimes of the doorbell from within. She'll wake Mother up if she's not careful.

'Hello,' I say in what I hope is an innocent manner. 'Can I help?'

The policewoman jumps in surprise, takes her finger off the button and turns and looks at me and then looks up at the suited man next to her. She is square; square face, square body and a very unflattering square haircut that only just covers her ears. On the large side but not supersize like I used to be, just normally fat. I'm not being judgemental about her weight – how could I be when I used to be so fat myself – but I've never seen anyone so square, and well, cuboid.

'Miss Travis?' the man says unsmilingly, looking down at me.

'Guilty as charged.' I don't know what made me say it and he doesn't smile. I feel my face start to burn. Why the hell did I say that? Maybe I should just offer him my wrists so he can snap the handcuffs on right now and save time.

'I'm Detective Inspector Peters and this is WPC Roper.' He nods at the square policewoman. 'We need to talk to you. If would be better if we could come in rather than stand on the doorstep?' He clears his throat and attempts a tight-lipped smile. Although he's really old he's quite attractive in a battered sort of way, a faded Count Dracula type of handsome.

'What do you want to talk to me about?'

'It would be better if we come inside,' he insists.

'My Mother's very ill,' I say unconvincingly. 'I don't want her disturbed.'

'Of course, I quite understand.' DI Peters smiles. 'We can do it down at the station if you prefer.'

Now I know it's serious. My heart starts to race so loudly I'm sure they must be able to hear it beating guilty, guilty, guilty.

'Can I see your ID?' I'm dragging it out and playing for time, my mind in a whirl of panic. I don't want to let them in, somehow that'll make it all real. Perhaps if I pinch myself really hard I'll wake up.

'Of course.' He pulls his warrant card out of his inside jacket pocket and holds it in front of my face. 'Very sensible. You can't be too careful.'

I stare at it unseeingly for some minutes as I try to think. It could say his name was Donald Duck and I wouldn't know.

'Okay,' I say, nodding at the warrant card. 'It all looks in order. If you'll let me get through I'll open the door.'

DI Peters steps behind me and WPC Roper steps to one side and I squeeze next to her and put my key in the lock. I unlock the front door; fumbling around as if I'm wearing boxing gloves and I wonder if I look as guilty as I feel. It must be the laptop because I can't think what else it could be; Justin's fancy lawyer must be hot stuff to get the police onto me this quickly. It just shows that if you have the money and speak in the right accent you can get out of anything and get the police to jump through hoops.

I finally manage to get the door open and I usher them through into the hall in front of me. The key seems to be stuck in the lock and I wiggle it around but I can't get it out. Why don't I confess right now and get it over with? I may as well, I couldn't look guiltier if I tried. They stand impassively and watch as I finally manage to wrench the key out of the lock. I think I've bent it.

'Go through, go through.' I wave in the direction of the lounge door. DI Peters nods at the WPC and they go in and I follow after them like a lamb to the slaughter.

'Please, sit down.'

They both choose to sit in the two armchairs facing the sofa which means I'll have to sit on the sofa opposite them.

'Cup of tea?' I offer, desperately hoping I can escape to the kitchen for a while.

'No thank you.' DI Peters shakes his head, unsmiling. WPC Roper says nothing and looks at her feet.

I give in and my legs crumple as I sit down onto the sofa facing them. The sun is streaming through the lounge window and I squint at them. It's very quiet and I have to stop myself from trying to fill the gap by gabbling. Actually, it's too quiet; no distant thrum of the television coming from Mother's room upstairs. I suspect she's turned it off so she can hear what's being said; she must have heard us come in and the doorbell was ringing for ages. She's probably lying down with her ear to the floor right this minute.

'Miss Travis,' DI Peters begins. 'We're making enquiries regarding a crime that may have been committed. Please understand that at this stage you are not under arrest and do not have to answer any questions if you choose not to. However, we hope that you will be willing to help us with our enquiries. Do you understand?'

I nod, mute. That's it then, they must know about Justin's laptop. Will I go to prison? It would be a first offence and what would they charge me with? Fraudulent use of a credit card? Opening an email account in someone else's name? Maybe I could plead mitigating circumstances; play the fat card. Except I'm not fat anymore so I can't. I thought I was being so clever and I'm just an idiot.

'Okay, Miss Travis. I understand that you work as a cleaner for Moppers Homeclean, is that correct?'

'Yes, that's right.'

'And how long have you worked there?'

'Let me see,' I gaze into the distant as if mentally calculating how long, 'Just over five months.'

He nods and in the ensuing silence I hear the

scratch of WPC Roper's pen as she scribbles in her notebook. Is she writing down everything I say? I fight the urge to repeat my answers slowly so she can get everything down properly. Part of me acknowledges the fact that I may be slightly hysterical or about to have a nervous breakdown. Or a heart attack. I could definitely have a heart attack.

'And do you clean at the house of a Mr Justin Willoughby and a Miss Bella Somerton?'

'Yes, that's right.' My voice sounds very squeaky and small and I have no idea whether I'm going to deny all knowledge or confess everything. I pray for an interruption; for the phone to ring or someone to knock at the door or Mother to shout for me. Anything to stop the questions. Maybe I'll just get a suspended sentence for a first offence. It's always in the papers that the prisons are full to bursting. Or maybe they'll want to make an example of me. Yes, I think they will. I'll probably be old by the time they let me out.

'Is it correct that a Mrs Rita Williams took you to Mr Willoughby and Miss Somerton's house on January 28th of this year for a training session, on your first day with Moppers?'

'She did, Doris Winterbourne came too.' I can't see what that's got to do with anything.

'Is it also correct that you've been cleaning Mr Willoughby's house while Mrs Williams was absent from work though sickness?'

'Yes.'

'Every week?'

'Yes.'

'What about last week? Did you go there last

219

week?'

'No. Not last week. Rita came back to work so she did it last week.' A sudden thought occurs to me; maybe I could blame Rita. I dismiss the thought immediately; any self-respecting IT geek will spot the dates I put the porn stuff on Justin's laptop in a jiffy and they won't tally up with Rita being there. Although I could use it as a delaying tactic while I think of something else.

'So, you're quite sure that you didn't go to Mr Willoughby and Miss Somerton's house last Monday?'

'No.'

'But you've been there today?'

'Well yes, because Rita's off sick again.'

'Just to be clear, Miss Travis, you're saying that you definitely didn't go to Mr Willoughby and Miss Somerton's house last Monday?'

'No, I didn't,' I say emphatically. That's a lie. I *did* go there, but only for five minutes. I didn't touch Justin's laptop last week and I can't see that it matters that I went there but I've lied now so I can't change it or else everything else I say will look like a lie.

'You weren't perhaps,' DI Peters stares at me intently, 'visiting a friend nearby and popped in for moment?'

'No,' I lie again. I'm starting to get a very bad feeling about this. Very bad. Did someone see me? I think I should have told the truth now. I thought I was so good at this lying thing but someone must have seen me for him to be making such a thing about it and now I can't untangle myself from it.

'Okay.' DI Peters looks pointedly at WPC Roper and nods imperceptibly. She closes her notebook with an air of finality and stands up. DI Peters also stands up and I realise again how tall he is.

'I'm afraid Miss Travis, that I'm going to have to ask you to accompany me to the station to continue our questioning.'

'What? But why? There's no need, I can answer your questions here.'

'I'm afraid I must insist.'

'No,' I say, shaking my head. 'I can't. I can't leave Mother on her own.'

'Well then you leave me no option.' He clears his throat. 'Alison Travis, I'm arresting you on suspicion of the attempted murder of Rita Williams. You do not have to say anything, but it may harm your defence if you do not mention when questioned something which you later rely on in court. Anything you do say may be given in evidence.'

I gawp at him. Oh no. This isn't about Justin's laptop at all.

'It'll be better for you if you come willingly. I don't want to have to handcuff you. Is there anyone who can come in and look after your mother for you?'

'But...' I can't get my words out. Handcuffs? Oh God, could it be any worse?

'A neighbour perhaps?'

I get up from the sofa and turn towards the door. 'I'll have to go up and tell Mother what's happening. She'll worry and she won't understand, she's not well, you know...'

DI Peters steps in front of me blocking my way. 'I'm afraid that won't be possible, Miss Travis. Don't worry.' He looks at me not unkindly. 'WPC Roper will tell your mother that you're helping us with our enquiries. That's all she needs to know at the moment.'

He nods at WPC Roper and she disappears through the doorway and I hear the thump of her heavy footsteps going up the stairs. I stand frozen to the spot in shock; at any moment I expect to hear Mother shouting for me. What will WPC Roper think when she sees the dining room chair wedged under the door handle to Mother's room?

'But she'll want her dinner,' I say stupidly. 'I have to cook her dinner. I must be back for five o'clock.' I look at my watch; it's quarter to three. I left Mother sandwiches for lunch when I took her breakfast up this morning but she'll be wanting her dinner at her usual time.

'Is there a neighbour who can pop in and see to her? Or a relative?'

It hits me; I won't be back in time to cook Mother's dinner and I might not be back anytime soon. Cooking Mother's dinner and looking after her suddenly seems like the thing that I want to do most in the world.

'I don't have any relatives, it's just me and Mother.'

'If there's no one at all we can call Social Services.'

If there's one thing I'm sure of it's that I don't want Social Services in here. If I don't go to prison for attempted murder then Mother would tell Social Services everything and I'd definitely be locked up for embezzling money from her account and who knows what else; I'd definitely be going to prison then, Mother would make absolutely sure of it. Maybe I could ask Dolph to come and look after her; he thinks Mother's a nutcase but the fact that he's a gossip machine would override his fear of her and he'd break his neck to get in here and find out what's going on. He's not ideal but he's the lesser of two evils. Hopefully he'd think anything Mother said to him was complete rubbish as I've put it about that she has dementia. Yes. Dolph would be more than happy to get in here and find out I've been arrested so he could broadcast it. I'm just about to suggest this when we hear the heavy, rapid clomp of WPC Roper's footsteps reverberating through the house as she comes back downstairs and into the lounge. She stands in front of DI Peters for a moment to catch her breath. Her skin is ashen and I wonder if she's ill; is she really so unfit that running up the stairs has exhausted her? Really, she needs to get some weight off.

'Sir?' she says, breathlessly. 'I think you'd better come upstairs.'

Chapter 21

WPC Roper has made me a cup of tea. It's all wrong, much too strong with milk and lots of sugar and it's in the wrong cup; one of Mother's flowery china cups with a saucer. I want to tell her that I always have a mug and that I don't take milk or sugar and that in fact I'd really rather have coffee but the words won't come out, my mouth seems to have stopped working.

She's standing over me and staring down at me in her square way and because it's expected of me I take a sip from the cup. The cloying sweetness hits my tongue and for a second I think I'm going to be sick but I somehow manage to force myself to swallow it down. The action of swallowing is painful and it feels as if I have a hard lump of rock wedged in my throat. I place the cup back on the saucer on the coffee table with a shaking hand and lean back against the sofa. In that instant I decide that I will probably never drink tea again.

I notice that the lounge door is closed and DI Peters isn't here. WPC Roper moves away from me and stands in front of the door with her feet apart and her hands behind her back. She's trying to look impassive but not succeeding; she cannot disguise a look of disgust and horror on her plain, cuboid features. It's a look that I've seen many times on people's faces and it doesn't bother me because I'm used to it. But I am puzzled by it because it's been a while since anyone's looked at me like that. Why is she looking at me like that because I'm not supersize now, I'm normal, and I don't get those looks any more.

How did I get to be sitting here drinking tea made by someone else in my own home? I remember WPC Roper stomping upstairs and DI Peters standing in the doorway, stopping me from going to see Mother but after that there's a blankness, a void that I cannot recall. Did I faint? I can't remember.

I stare at the coffee table, tracing every detail of the rose pattern on the teacup and trying to remember what's happened. Something major has happened, I can sense it, and I'm sure if I sit here quietly for a while it'll all come back to me.

I remember answering questions and feeling frightened for some reason. I think I did faint, I remember now. There was a buzzing in my ears that got louder and louder and it got so loud that it turned into a banging noise as if someone were playing the drums in my head. And the louder the drums got the darker the room became.

Yes, that's it, I definitely fainted.

I have a memory of the coolness of someone's hand pressed to my forehead, gentle fingers holding my wrist, feeling for my pulse. *She'll be fine, it's the shock,* words spoken in a calm measured voice and then the voice of DI Peters thanking someone, a doctor. Doctor Beamish. It explains the vile sweet tea, the blankness of what's happened. I know that soon I will remember and that I don't want to.

I feel dazed and shaky and when I tear my gaze

225

from the teacup and look down at my hands in my lap, they lay there like strange appendages, sausages with fingernails. They don't look or feel like my hands, it's almost as if they're not attached to my body. I interlock my fingers and stretch them this way and that and then bring my hands to my face and press my fingers over my eyes and breathe deeply. I'm starting to feel better, I feel less bewildered, more together as if my mind and body have drifted apart but are now melding back together.

I look up as the sound of movement upstairs draws my attention, the low murmur of voices is followed by brisk footsteps on the stairs. WPC Roper is watching me from under her eyelashes, she sees me looking up at the ceiling as if it will provide me with answers. There are strangers in the house; Mother won't like it, we never have visitors. Who are they, these people – are there more police officers upstairs? For some reason I think there are, so something must have happened. I wonder if they've been into Mother's room and spoken to her, what did they think when they had to remove the dining chair from underneath the door handle?

I remember that soon I'll be taken to the police station. Something to do with Rita.

Attempted murder! I remember now, the questioning about visiting Bella's house, the lie that I told repeatedly that I thought so unimportant. How can they think I wanted to murder Rita? They've got it all wrong; it's all a terrible mistake. I'm sure they'll put the questioning off for another day because of what's happened.

What *has* happened? I know something has

happened but I can't remember what. Not the Rita thing, I remember that. There's something else, something important that I should remember.

I close my eyes and think; it's something to do with Mother. Has she been telling lies about me? Well, not lies, the truth; that I've kept her prisoner, a well looked after prisoner but a prisoner none the less.

No. It's not that. But it is something to do with Mother. And it must be something shocking for me to faint; I don't think I've ever fainted before. After the darkness closed in I remember falling but I don't think I hit the floor, I don't hurt anywhere and I can't feel any tender spots so somebody must have caught me. Thank God I'm not supersize anymore otherwise I could have killed whoever it was who caught me if I'd fallen on them.

Mother.

I remember. DI Peters told me that Mother is dead. I can't remember his exact words but he imparted the news to me in a sombre, sad voice; the sort of voice reserved for telling people bad news.

I think about it and decide that yes, that means they'll definitely put the questioning off for another day, a day when Mother hasn't died. The police aren't completely heartless, they won't want to interrogate someone who's just lost a close relative.

It was weird when DI Peters told me Mother had died and maybe it was the shock, but do you know what I thought when he told me? I thought; I won't have to worry about getting someone in to cook her dinner now; there's no need to bother Dolph and that's good because he won't be able to spread lots of gossip about me.

I don't think I said it out loud, at least I hope I didn't. DI Peters looked at me in that sad way and I remember thinking, why do you look so sad? You didn't even know her and if you did know her you certainly wouldn't be sad. I shouldn't have thought that, should I? She may be dead but she's still my mother, *I'm* the one who should be sad but I'm not, I'm relieved.

And free at last.

But I won't be free for long if I'm charged with attempted murder.

I can hear cars pulling up out in the street and I think the front door must be open. WPC Roper is planted firmly in front of the closed lounge door so I know there's no hope of me having a look to see what's going on. The sound of heavy boots clomping around in the hallway carries through the house and low voices of what I guess are more police officers coming into the house. The neighbours will be agog by now, there'll be no hiding the fact that something has happened at number six Duck Pond Lane, the rumour mills will be spinning like Topsy. And that includes Bella's grandparents.

I know that we have to wait for the police pathologist to arrive before they can move Mother so someone must have told me that but I can't remember who. There seems to be an awful lot of police here, perhaps that's usual for a sudden death. Not so sudden when I think about it; Mother had been complaining of a headache for the past few days so I'm guessing she's had another stroke. I wonder how long she's been dead? She was okay when I left her this morning. Would it have been a swift death? If I'd been here instead of at Bella's when it happened and had called an ambulance would she have survived? Before I can stop it that nasty little voice chips in: *aren't you glad you weren't here?*

I look over at WPC Roper. 'Can I see her?' I surprise myself by asking, my voice croaky and quiet as if it hasn't been used for a long time.

She flushes and answers me without meeting my gaze because for some reason she doesn't want to look at me.

'I'm afraid that's not possible at the moment.'

'Why not? She's my mother. I've a right to see her.'

WPC Roper clears her throat. She looks uncomfortable but she doesn't answer me.

'I'm her daughter,' I go on, 'I should be allowed to see my own mother.'

WPC Roper looks down at her large feet and says nothing. I wonder briefly if I'm in the middle of some horrible nightmare; the sort where you try to run but you can't move or your legs move but you stay in the same place, like jogging on the spot. Or you scream but no sound comes out of your mouth, just a horrible choking sensation.

But I'm only trying to fool myself. I know really that it's not a dream from which I can wake up, it's all too horribly real.

I ask myself if I really want to see Mother. The answer is that I don't know but I do know that I don't want to sit here while the police are stomping around our house, *my* house, and I don't want to wait to be told what to do. I feel a spike of anger and indignation; shouldn't the police be suggesting that I contact a relative, or a friend, to offer me some support and sympathy instead of leaving me sitting alone on the sofa with only an uncommunicative policewoman for company? Is it really fair to expect me to sit here with a sour faced WPC watching me when I've just lost my mother? Yes, I decide, my indignation growing. I will demand that they let me contact Doris. She's my friend, she'll come even though she hates the police and calls them *the filth*.

I listen as multiple heavy footsteps descend the stairs. There's a brief moment of quiet which is followed by a burst of activity from the hallway, the sound of the front door being closed and then opened and the shuffle and thump of footsteps as if something is being manoeuvred through the doorway. Muffled voices and shouts and then the thud of car doors being slammed in the street. I know what this is; they're taking Mother away. Where will they take her? Not to the hospital. It's too late for the hospital.

WPC Roper has heard the commotion too and she visibly straightens up, pushes her shoulders back and glances back at the closed lounge door. She's waiting for it to open, willing someone to come in and relieve her from the burden of me and my questions.

She moves aside just as the door opens and DI Peters steps into the room.

'We're ready to leave now.' He looks at WPC Roper when he says it but I think he's talking to me as well.

WPC Roper comes over and stands in front of me and I think I should get up and show them out, even in the midst of grief I still have good manners. Okay, I'm not in the throes of grief but they don't know that. I'm glad they're going at last, I need time to get my thoughts in order. I pull myself up from the sofa, wondering if my shaky legs will hold me and, surprisingly, they do. I must be recovering now, getting over the shock of it all. I stand still for a moment to make sure the buzzing noise doesn't return and send me back into black forgetfulness. When I'm quite sure I'm stable I turn to DI Peters.

'When should I come in to the station?'

'You need to come now, Miss Travis.' DI Peters answers from the doorway as WPC Roper turns away, avoiding me and my questions.

'Now? But my mother's just passed away.'

'Yes, and I'm very sorry for your loss but I'm afraid you need to accompany us to the station now.'

I remember then, with horror, the talk of arrest and handcuffs. But surely, they'll allow me to take someone with me.

'Can I call someone?' I speak directly to DI Peters hoping he won't ignore me like WPC Roper has. I want to call Doris, to see concern on the face of my only friend. She'll come, I know she will; I want her reassuring gruffness, her assurance that she'll look after me, her arms thrown around me while she pulls me toward her and thumps my back and tells me everything is going to be alright.

Is it my imagination or does DI Peters look embarrassed? Can policemen look embarrassed? I must be imagining it.

'When we get to the station,' he says, turning to leave the room.

'I think I'd like my friend, Doris, to come with me. I've just lost my mother,' I say in disbelief.

DI Peters stops in the doorway and turns back to face me.

'When we get to the station, Miss Travis. You have a right to a telephone call when we get to the station.'

And that's when I realise and it all makes horrifying sense.

They think that I've killed Mother as well as Rita.

Chapter 22

They asked me if I wanted a solicitor. I said *I haven't done anything wrong so why would I need a solicitor?* They – DI Peters and another policeman, a Sergeant Stephens, didn't answer me. DI Peters seems quite nice but Sergeant Stephens doesn't; short, skinny and decidedly rodent like, he arrived in the room in a fug of stale cigarette smoke, briefly and unsmilingly introduced himself to me, nodded at DI Peters and then the two of them both went out and left me in here on my own. I wonder if they're going to do good cop bad cop on me or have I watched too many police dramas?

They've told me that I have to call someone or else a solicitor will be arranged on my behalf. I definitely don't want a stranger so I thought for a while about who I should call and I decided that maybe Doris wasn't the best person to ask for. She's not a solicitor and I also have a sneaking suspicion that she might have *previous,* if you know what I mean, so that might not be very helpful. There's also the chance that she'd freak out if I asked her.

Since the horrific journey from Duck Pond Lane and then Peters and Stephens brief visits I've been left alone in this room with pea coloured walls and no windows. The only furniture is a teak effect Formica topped, metal-legged table with four matching chairs arranged around it. A very young WPC came in and provided me with a cup of tea and then left immediately.

Although I was only in the police car for about fifteen minutes it felt like forever. Every time we stopped at a traffic light or slowed down I tried to make myself as small as possible so that no one could see me if they looked in. I even took my ponytail out so I could pull my hair around my face and try to hide behind it. It was awful and all I kept thinking was, *they must think I'm a murderer if they've arrested me.*

I'm sitting with my hands linked together on the table and staring at them. I'm very aware of the camera mounted in the corner of the room. This may be just to film my interview but I'm taking no chances; I don't want to display any sort of behaviour that could indicate guilt.

Although I don't know what sort of behaviour that is – they could think I'm a cold-blooded killer for not displaying any emotion. I don't know so I'll pretend to be in shock. Although I don't have to pretend, really.

There's a double tape machine which takes up a third of the table. I know this is to tape our interview, one copy for them and one for me. I haven't watched EastEnders for nothing. My mobile phone was taken away from me at the front desk although part of me wonders if they're allowed to do that. Maybe this is part of the softening up process, maybe they're trying to panic me by leaving me alone. If only they knew that I've been alone for all of my life.

I do feel a lot better than I did and I've managed to calm down, the initial shock when I realised that they thought I'm some sort of serial killer has gone now. I just have to convince them that it's all been a terrible, silly mistake. I'm not sure how I feel about Mother dying. I can't quite believe she's gone. I should probably feel sad about it but at the moment I don't. I'm too busy trying not to be charged with murder. Maybe I'll feel sorry about her death later. Maybe I'll miss her later. I doubt it and for now I'm not going to think about her.

I've made my mind up that I'm going to call Gerald, he's a solicitor although I don't know if he does criminal stuff; I think he's more house sales and wills but he's the only solicitor I know. I've thought about this long and hard because obviously he's going to find out that I'm a liar as he doesn't know that I'm a cleaner. And looking a liar is not a good start when you want someone to defend you. But actually, I think I could probably convince him that I told him what I did for a living when we went on our date. After all, he wasn't really listening because he was too busy talking about himself.

But whether he believes me or not I think I can handle that, more to the point I think I can handle *him*.

My head is starting to pound and I'm tired of sitting here waiting for someone to come and interrogate me. What would a normal person who'd just lost their beloved mother do in my situation? Would they sit meekly and wait? I don't think they would, they'd be demanding answers.

Decision made, I walk over to the door and rap sharply on the window to try and attract someone's attention. I try the door handle and rattle it. It's locked.

After a few minutes of my knuckle rapping a uniformed policeman appears at the door window and then unlocks and opens the door.

'What's the problem?' He raises one eyebrow and has a slight sneer on his face. No *madam* or *Miss Travis*, it seems that I'm to be denied those niceties now I'm suspected of murder.

'I'd like my telephone call.'

'If you sit down I'll arrange it,' he says flatly, already closing the door as he speaks. I'm left staring at the closed door. I've been found guilty already.

I sit down and drum my fingers on the table, frustrated that my fate is in the hands of other people. The thought of being incarcerated in a prison brings me out in a cold sweat; the thought of not being able to go out when I want and being told what to do all of the time is unbearable. Mother imprisoned me for years but at least I eventually escaped and just when I can see complete freedom on the horizon it could all be snatched away from me.

The door clicks and Sergeant Stephens comes into the room.

'If you come with me you can make your telephone call.'

I get up without a word and follow him, he must have come straight from the smoking shelter because he leaves a trail of stale cigarette smoke in his wake. He stops in front of the desk and nods at the phone extension on the desk.

'You've got five minutes. You have to put a nine in front.'

I wait for him to move but he folds his arms and

236

stands watching. There's a bespectacled receptionist sitting behind the desk typing rapidly on a keyboard. She doesn't look up as I turn my back on Stephens and pick the phone up. I realise that I don't know Gerald's phone number.

'I need my phone to look up the phone number.' I turn around to face Sergeant Stephens.

'Who are you trying to ring?'

'My solicitor.'

'We've got all of the solicitor's numbers. Who is it?'

'Thompsons.'

'Zoe, you've got Thompsons on your list, haven't you?' He completely ignores me and speaks to the receptionist behind the desk.

She stops typing for a moment, spins her swivel chair around to face the wall, looks at a list pinned to the notice board and reads out a number.

'Sorry, could you say that again?' She read it so quickly I couldn't punch the numbers in quick enough. She purses her lips and reads it again, very slowly, and I punch the numbers in and hope desperately that Gerald isn't out of the office. Will I be allowed another call if he's not there or is this the only one I'll get? After three rings the phone is answered by the snooty tones of Eunice. I ask for Gerald and realise that I have my fingers crossed.

'Putting you through.' Thank God, he's there.

'Gerald Thompson.'

'Gerald?' I query. 'It's Alison.'

'Hi Alison,' he says warmly, sounding pleased to hear from me and I remember that I told him I was away on business and would contact him when I got back. It dawns on me that he's not going to believe I told him I was a cleaner. Too bad, there's nothing I can do about it now. He must think I'm ringing up to arrange a date.

'Hey, how are you, how was your trip?'

Yep. Apparently, he did listen. So what did I go and do?

I burst into tears.

Gerald is on his way to the police station and I'm back in the interview room, locked in. I don't know why I burst into tears but, on reflection, I think that was probably the very best thing I could have done, helpless, grieving female and all that. I had to hand the phone over to Sergeant Stephens to explain the situation as I was blubbing so much. He looked at me with absolute disgust before having a short, terse conversation with Gerald before hanging up. He never spoke a word to me and ushered me back in here with a hand on my back which was almost a shove. I think he's taken a massive dislike to me which obviously isn't going to help my case.

I've stopped crying now and I wish I had a comb and a bit of make-up with me because I'm sure I look a wreck and not a bit like the glamorous creature that Gerald knows. It's probably a good thing that there aren't any mirrors in here to make me feel any worse. I'm wondering how long he'll take to get here when the door clicks behind me and I hear Gerald's voice as he comes in.

'....I'll need some time alone with my client.' He shuts the door and walks over to me. He looks just as gorgeous as ever and I wonder what he must think of the train wreck standing in front of him. For no good reason that I can think of I stand up from the chair.

'You poor thing, what the hell are they thinking of?' Gerald shocks me by taking me in his arms and holding me tight. I relax in his embrace and allow myself to be held.

'They think I killed someone.' I sniff. 'They think I killed Mummy.'

'Barbaric. Absolutely barbaric.' He pats my back reassuringly, 'Don't worry I'll soon have you out of here.'

We stay like this for several minutes and then Gerald gently releases his arms and stands back and looks at me.

He brushes a stray hair back from my forehead and smiles sadly at me and I realise that he's enjoying playing a knight in shining armour. He pulls the chair out next to me and sits down and I sit and turn to face him.

'What have they told you?'

'That I've been arrested for attempted murder.' I shake my head in disbelief. 'A lady called Rita, she works where I work.'

He looks at me in concern and nods.

'Gerald,' I say, stifling a sob, 'I have a confession to make, I lied to you about my job, I'm not really a food writer at all. I'm a cleaner.'

Gerald doesn't look too surprised and I guess that the police have already told him. Of course he'd know what they're charging me with. I hurriedly continue before he can think too much about it.

'And I feel so, so bad about that, but I was only trying to impress you. I'm not really a liar, it's just,' I squeeze out another tear and it rolls down my cheek, 'that you're so successful, and well, amazing, I thought you wouldn't want to know me if you knew the truth. Cleaning was the only job that I could get that fitted in with caring for mummy.'

Gerald takes my hand and holds it gently between both of his.

'Of course I don't think you're a liar and none of that matters now. The main thing is that we get this sorted out and they let you go home.'

I sniff and smile bravely and gaze adoringly into Gerald's eyes.

The shuffle of feet and voices interrupt this touching moment and DI Peters and Sergeant Stephens enter the room. Gerald quickly lets go of my hand and bends down and makes a show of rummaging in his briefcase. It's been noted though; the hand holding, I can tell.

There's a lot of scraping of chair legs and Peters and Stephens deposit themselves in the seats opposite us, arranging the files they're brought with them onto the desk. Gerald produces a large, thick writing pad and places it carefully on the desk in front of him and puts a chunky, expensive looking pen on top.

Stephens opens his file and produces two cassette tapes in plastic wrapping. He snaps the plastic from them and slots both of them into the recorder, presses a button and a red-light glows on the front of the device.

'For the benefit of the tape please state your full name and address.'

He must mean me, he's looking at me.

'Alison Travis, six Duck Pond Lane.'

'Miss Travis. Is it correct that you are employed by Moppers Homeclean Ltd of Frogham?'

'It is.'

'Is it also correct that on January 28th of this year you visited Mr Justin Willoughby's house with a Mrs Rita Williams?'

I open my mouth to say yes when Gerald stops me by holding his hand up.

'You don't have to answer that.'

I've already told them that I was there so they know but on the other hand, I think Gerald doesn't want me to answer.

'No comment.' I say and I sense Gerald's approval.

Stephen's lips press tightly together.

'Is it also true that you visited the Willoughby's house on Monday last when Rita Williams was cleaning there?'

'No comment.' I'm getting the hang of this now.

'We have a witness who saw you entering the Willoughby's house on Monday last.'

Gerald sighs theatrically.

'My client is not going to answer any more questions until you provide us with the details of the alleged charge and who this witness is.' He twirls the chunky pen in his fingers. 'In fact, I've a mind to make a complaint to the relevant authorities about your treatment of someone who has just suffered the loss of their mother.'

'At the moment Miss Travis is helping us with our enquiries; we arrested her on suspicion of murder as she would not come willingly to the station.' Stephens looks livid; his lips are pressed tightly together and I

241

can see his nostrils flaring with the effort of controlling what I guess to be a hair trigger temper.

Gerald makes a snorting noise of disgust through his nose.

Stephens looks at DI Peters who nods.

'The alleged charge is the attempted murder of Rita Williams by poisoning on January 28th and May 28th.'

'And what evidence do you have that my client is implicated?'

'Miss Travis had access to Mrs Williams' belongings on or about January 28th. Miss Travis was also seen by a witness outside the Willoughby's house last Monday.'

'And that's it? That's the extent of your evidence?' Gerald affects an amazed expression on his face. 'You dragged my recently bereaved client into this station to question her without any substantive evidence?'

'It's on record that Mrs Williams has twice been hospitalised and nearly died on the second occasion after poison was administered.'

'What sort of poison?' Gerald snaps.

'Peanuts.'

'I'm sorry, I thought you said peanuts.' Gerald says sarcastically.

'I did. Mrs Williams has a very severe peanut allergy and the evidence points to Miss Travis tampering with Mrs William's water bottle and introducing traces of peanut into the water.'

'Fingerprints?' Gerald asks, his confidence brimming over.

A sheepish look is exchanged between the detectives.

242

'No, I thought not.' Gerald is shaking his head emphatically. 'You have no evidence and I want my client released immediately.'

'Miss Travis was seen outside the Willoughby's house last Monday.'

'That's not evidence. Was she seen going into the house?'

'No.' Stephens sighs as Peters watches me intently, waiting for a reaction. I keep my face passive.

'Then you have nothing.'

'We have a statement from the manager at Moppers Homeclean that Miss Travis was insistent that she replace Mrs Williams at the Willoughby's house. Unusually insistent, we were told.'

Veronica. The cow.

'So,' Gerald pauses and looks at me and smiles and I realise that he's enjoying himself immensely. 'What you have is hearsay and gossip that my client was so desperate to clean Mr Willoughby's house that she poisoned a work colleague.' He laughs mockingly. 'Hardly a motive is it? Is my client the only one who had access to Mrs William's bag?' Gerald holds his hand up as Stephens opens his mouth to answer. 'It was a rhetorical question Sergeant, of course she wasn't. Now, I demand that you bring this interview to an end immediately and return my client's belongings to her.'

DI Peters clears his throat.

'Mrs Williams is insistent that she saw Miss Travis out of the window as she was dusting the windowsill.'

'Mrs Williams, the alleged victim?' Gerald shakes his head. 'So you don't have a witness at all, then.' He picks up his notepad and puts it in his briefcase. 'Just one person's word against another.'

'There's no denying that Mrs Williams was hospitalised on two occasions.'

'And yet she waited four months after the first occasion to make a complaint.'

'It was only when Mrs Williams remembered that she saw Miss Travis last week that she made the connection with what had happened in January. That was when she realised that her bottle of water had been tampered with.'

'Flimsy in the extreme, she may well have eaten something she shouldn't have by mistake.'

'There is also the matter of Mrs Travis's sudden death.' His hair trigger temper now perilously close to firing, Sergeant Stephens almost shouts at Gerald.

'Sudden death? You seriously…' Gerald leans across the desk to stare straight into Stephens rat-like features. '…think that my client, Mrs Travis's devoted daughter and carer, had anything to do with an elderly lady's not unexpected demise?'

They eyeball each other for several moments before DI Peters quietly clears his throat.

'There is the matter of the chair.' He says gently.

Gerald sits back in his chair and turns his attention to DI Peters.

'The chair?' Gerald says in a puzzled way.

'The chair,' Sergeant Stephens says nastily, 'that was wedged under the door handle of your client's mother's door so that she couldn't get out.'

Oh God. The chair. I'd almost forgotten about that.

Gerald turns to me with a shocked look on his face.

'It was for her own safety,' I say in a measured voice. 'She was getting very forgetful and confused. On one occasion she had dragged herself out of bed and I was afraid she might fall down the stairs if she managed to get out of her room.'

I watch Gerald's reaction as I speak and I can tell from his expression that he believes me. Totally.

'So, a perfectly reasonable explanation. Is that it? Do you think this is an acceptable reason to detain my client? Do you have any actual evidence that Mrs Travis's death wasn't natural causes?'

Sergeant Stephen's opens his mouth to speak but Gerald stops him with a glare.

'You do *not*. You have no evidence and absolutely no justification to hold my client for a moment longer.'

DI Peters quietly closes the file in front of him.

'I take it we're done here?' Gerald demands.

'You can go.' Sergeant Stephens says to me ungraciously, 'But we may have further questions for you at a later date.'

'No, you won't.' Gerald stands up, 'Think yourselves lucky that my client isn't making a complaint against you.'

I stand up next to Gerald and try not to smile.

It seems that I've got away with it.

Chapter 23

I didn't intend to kill her.

Honestly.

My only defence is that I wasn't in my right mind, I wasn't thinking straight; I hadn't been thinking straight for a long time. Also, it was ridiculously easy, *she* made it so easy.

And just to be clear, we're talking about Rita, not Mother. No, Mother was nothing to do with me, her death was sheer coincidence and completely natural. A stroke, according to the post mortem; to be expected, apparently, in someone of Mother's age with her medical history.

That's not to say that the thought of murdering Mother never crossed my mind. It did. But only ever fleetingly, and in very low moments, because I'm not a murderer.

I just wanted to make Rita ill enough so that she'd stay off work so that I could take over her shifts at Bella's. I knew that she had a peanut allergy but so did the whole world because she had to tell *everyone*, all of the time. But I thought she was exaggerating when she said the slightest trace could kill her, I didn't think a tiny little smear would kill her and it didn't, did it? And that's all it was, a trace; the merest wipe of peanut oil on the inside of a bottle of water purchased from Foodco.

It was so ridiculously easy; I knew which bottles of water she always bought because she was always flashing them in everyone's face (value range, six small bottles for fifty-nine pence). I bought some myself and then I just had to swap my bottle for hers – it was too easy. She always had at least two bottles rattling around in that humungous handbag and there's no way she could see what I'd done because the value range only have normal screw on tops and you couldn't even tell I'd opened it after I screwed it back on tightly. It's not as if she was even looking, anyway.

The police were wrong about me doing it the first time that Rita took us to Bella's though. The idea didn't even occur to me until afterwards and then all I had to do was wait until the Friday when all of the cleaners went into the office to give in their timesheets. It's always a bit of a crush and Rita would insist of leaving that stupid handbag of hers lying around, usually getting in everyone's way and taking up one of the few chairs in the office. A quick scan of the room to make sure no one was looking at me and then I simply swapped my bottle for hers.

The police were right about me being at Bella's last week when Rita was there cleaning; I was in and out of there in less than five minutes and the job was done. A bit unfortunate that Rita saw me from the window but it's only her word against mine isn't it? And she couldn't have actually seen me go *into* the house if she was upstairs in the front bedroom, she must have only thought about it afterwards and put two and two together. I am surprised though, that she thought it was me, that she joined up the dots. I really didn't think she was that bright.

Anyway, I've just remembered, as they say, that I was out running that morning so I may well have passed Bella's house and not given it much thought at the time.

I do feel sorry about it though because I'm not a complete monster. I'm relieved that Rita's okay and that there's no long-term damage. I knew she was the sort that would never be far from her EpiPen. All the same, she might want to think about who she tells about her allergy in the future, might be best if she didn't bang on about it to all and sundry because not everyone's as nice as me.

Gerald's been an absolute revelation; when he's in solicitor mode he's very impressive and much more attractive than when he's blathering on endlessly and boringly in a social environment. I could quite fancy him when he's getting me off a murder charge, he's quite masterful.

The evidence was flimsy to say the least but of course I couldn't see that in my state of panic. In fact, they didn't have any evidence as such, but I have a feeling that the police thought I would crumble and incriminate myself– and I so nearly did. The only thing that still concerns me a bit is if Justin goes to the police about his laptop; things could get very sticky if that happens and I'm not sure how I could lie my way out of that.

It's unlikely though; I've heard no more from the police since I was released and it's over two weeks now, so I'm optimistic. I'll just have to keep my fingers crossed that Justin doesn't decide to try and prove his innocence. And I need to keep Gerald sweet too in case I need him to ride to the rescue again. Hopefully Justin will take his suspension from work like a man, do a bit of grovelling to Bella and everything will go back to how it was. I think it will; I've started to include Bella's house on my daily running route and on the last two occasions as I went by I saw Justin's car was parked on the driveway. So I think she's going to take him back if she hasn't done so already. She has a level of credit card debt that is frankly unmanageable on her salary so I'm sure she'll forgive him. I thank my lucky stars that I didn't put child porn on his laptop or the police definitely would be involved and then my carefully constructed house of lies would all come tumbling down.

I can look back on my actions dispassionately now, the way I've behaved seems very strange to me and if it did ever come to court I think I'd have to plead diminished responsibility. In other words: I went a bit mad. I couldn't even explain why I did what I did to Justin, or what I hoped to achieve by it.

I suppose the years of caring for Mother took their toll. I'm not a psychologist but I think that my obsession with Bella was a way of changing myself and my life and that if it hadn't been her I would have found someone else to fixate on and use as a role model.

I don't consider that I've been cruel to Mother, I still looked after her even though I made sure she couldn't come downstairs. She had her television and her magazines and cooked meals, all of the home comforts. I don't feel guilty, and anyway nobody knows that she was basically a prisoner so that's all fine. I was a prisoner for most of my life and definitely for the last ten years so is it any wonder I went a bit mad?

Luckily, no lasting damage has been done, to me, that is. Although I will have to be very careful in the future. Because I'm definitely not the person that I thought I was; I spent most of my life thinking I was weak and stupid because that's what Mother kept telling me but of course I'm not like that at all. In fact, the things that I'm capable of are rather frightening so I've given myself a good talking to and made a promise that I'll behave. I need to stop the lying too.

Unless it's absolutely necessary of course.

Mother's funeral hasn't happened yet; some sort of backlog at the crematorium, too many people dying apparently. It's going to be next Monday and Doris and Gerald have promised to come and support me which is really sweet of them. In a way it's lucky that it's been delayed because Doris had a week's holiday booked in Marbella (*y'know, on that little island, Spain I fink it's called* she said, I didn't have the heart to tell her it's not an island.) She wouldn't have been back in time if the funeral had been any sooner. I gave her the green dress to take on holiday and she was delighted with it and says she's going to wear it with her Primark wedges.

I'm still employed by Moppers but I'm on compassionate leave at the moment. I've decided I'm going to leave after the funeral but I'm not going to tell Veronica yet. I'm being paid full wages which is unusual but I know that's only because Veronica feels guilty for dobbing me into the police as a murderer. Doris says Veronica looks very sheepish whenever my name is mentioned so I've told her to mention me at

250

every opportunity to make her squirm.

Gerald has got over his initial shock at finding out that I'm a cleaner and is keen for me to get a *job more suitable to my talents,* he's even offered to ask around his friends to see if they have anything suitable. He's been visiting me a lot – I had to let him into the house so unfortunately, he's seen the hideous seventies décor and horrific furniture – and he's been very kind. He did have a funny look on his face when he saw the state of the place; he looked around as if I lived in a museum.

He also doesn't know I used to be jumbo-sized and I'm certainly not going to tell him; there's only so much truth he can cope with. I think the thought of me as hugely fat would be a step too far for him. No, I'll keep that to myself I think, there's no need for him to know. We haven't progressed our relationship any further yet and he's not pushing it as I'm still grieving, apparently. He's being all gallant and has told me he's prepared to *wait until I'm ready.* I think he's quite enjoying his role as my hero. Also, he's not used to having someone who doesn't jump straight into bed with him though I'm sure the novelty will wear off once I sleep with him.

He's going to help me put the house up for sale after the funeral and says I should get a really good price for it even though it needs completely updating. I'm going to buy myself a nice modern apartment and bank the rest of the money, which if I get what he thinks the house is worth will be a huge amount. Realistically, there's no rush to get a job, I could have a few years off and do some travelling.

But I don't think I will, I think I need to channel

my energies into some sort of career; too much time on my hands and I could get into mischief and I don't want to go down that road again.

Once I have a buyer I'm going to arrange for one of those house clearance companies to come in and clear the house. Apart from my clothes and laptop I'm getting rid of everything, the whole lot. I hate this house and I can't wait to leave it. Maybe a young couple like those at number five will buy it and dispel the miserable ghosts of Mother and my grandparents and the old, fat me.

I hope so.

When Gerald brought me home from the police station I'm sure every curtain in the street was twitching. I decided the best form of defence was attack so I waited for a few days and then I strolled along to Dolph's and knocked at his door. He was delighted to see me although he tried to hide it and looked all compassionate and caring, but I could practically hear the cogs of the rumour mill grinding around his brain. He took me indoors and plied me with tea and some horrible lemon pie that Brian had made and I sobbed convincingly on his kitchen table.

I told him everything, the truth actually, about how I'd been arrested and Mother had just died and how absolutely awful it all was and how it was all a huge mistake. I stopped short of suggesting police brutality (remembering my promise to myself to stop lying) but let's just say that the police didn't come out of it very well. Dolph was horrified and I was still there when Brian came home from work and he joined in being horrified. Dolph then insisted that I let him cut my hair for me, *to make me feel better* and he made a lovely job of it; I might even start using him now Mother's not here.

Anyway, by the time I left, Dolph had all of the information that he needed to set everyone straight on what had really happened and I'm sure he lost no time in putting the word out. I have noticed over the last week that the neighbours are giving me friendly waves and saying hello instead of avoiding me or cutting me dead.

There's just the funeral to get out of the way now; I can't say that I'm looking forward to it and I did actually think *do I really have to go?* It's not as if I need to be there is it? They could just shove her in the burner and dispense with the service as far as I'm concerned. If Doris and Gerald weren't so insistent on coming then I really wouldn't bother. I can't pretend to myself that I care that Mother's dead even though I'll put on the pretence in front of others, which is a form of lying which I said I wouldn't do but it'll be the last time. Probably.

If I'm completely honest I'm relieved Mother's dead, it means I can move on and start my life again, start to live my life how it should be. How it should have been except that now I'm quite rich.

So, all in all, life's looking very positive and I have lots to look forward to. Funny, isn't it? This time last year I was supersize and now I'm super fit. A chance sighting of Bella in Foodco changed my life which just seems incredible, doesn't it?

And I'm free of Mother, which also seems incredible.

I feel quite affectionate towards Foodco although obviously I rarely shop there now; mostly I buy my food from Marks and Spencer. Although I did pop in there yesterday because M&S shut at eight and I was coming back from my run at about half-past-nine and I remembered I'd run out of raspberries for my breakfast. I popped in and was on my way to the till when the sound of laughter caught my attention.

Nasty, loud, mocking laughter and when I looked across the supermarket I saw that the laughter was coming from four teenage girls who looked to be about fifteen. They were all walking along in an exaggerated way, arms out to the side, legs bent with their heads down and shuffling along. Intrigued, I followed them and as I got a bit closer I could see there was a man in front of them. He was a bit younger than me but he was as fat, or maybe even fatter, than I used to be.

Those girls were mimicking him but the worst thing was that he knew it; I could tell by his ears, they were beetroot red. And they were getting closer and closer to him and they didn't care that he knew they were laughing at him because he knew he was fair game because he was so huge. He was shuffling along in the way I used to; head down, eyes down, thinking it would somehow make him less visible.

I felt for him, I really did (see, I'm *not* a monster) and I wanted to help him. I wanted to tell him, *look, just because you're super fat it doesn't mean that you don't deserve politeness or respect, you're still a person so put your head up and be proud of who you are and people won't be so quick to laugh at you. Don't apologise for existing.*

But I knew he wouldn't listen, the same way I wouldn't have listened. If anyone had come up to me in Foodco and said things like that when I was fat I'd

254

have thought they were making fun of me and trying to embarrass me. So what I did do was speed up a bit until I was right behind those four girls, and my little hand basket on wheels, those ones that I always thought looked so chic when other people pulled them? Well, I swung it around in front of me and somehow, I pushed it a bit too hard and it sort of went into the backs of their legs and the one on the end, the ringleader, she nearly fell over.

When they'd recovered themselves those four girls turned around and looked at me and they looked a spiteful lot; not afraid of anyone. I thought; they'll start on me now but I can take it, you don't frighten me.

'Sorry,' I said cheerfully, in a *not sorry* voice.

It was very strange. They all took a good, long look at me and then after a moment they looked at each other uncertainly and turned around and walked away.

I think I heard one of them say *bitch*, or it might have been *witch*.

And I thought, *no, you're wrong.*
I'm fat girl slim.

One last thing…

Thank you so much for reading this book. I really do appreciate it. I am an Indie Author, not backed by a big publishing company, so every time a reader downloads one of my books, I am genuinely thrilled. I've worked hard to eliminate any typos and errors, but if you spot any, please let me know: marinajohnson2017@outlook.com

If you have enjoyed this book please leave a review on Amazon and/or Goodreads, and if you think your friends would enjoy reading it, please share it with them.

Many thanks
Marina

Email: marinajohnson2017@outlook.com
Twitter: @mjohnsonwriter